THE LANGUID
BELLY OF
THE BEAST

JS CARTER GILSON
THE LANGUID BELLY OF THE BEAST

Cavia *Porcellus*

Nashua, nh

Cavia Porcellus
Nashua, NH

ISBN 978-1-95504-501-8

Design by Cavia Porcellus.
Cover features illustrations furnished by Pond 5,
http://www.pond5.com/

For Mom & Dad,
who never said
not to do this.

At night I drink myself to sleep
and pretend I don't care that you're not here with me.
Cause it's so much easier to handle
all my problems if I'm too far out to sea.

—*R.E.M.*, (Don't Go Back to) Rockville

1

Inez needed a vacation. She was just finishing her last job, one that had, remarkably, failed to kill her. She was overseeing the detachment of the cargo hold at the Company docking station above the new Free Earth colony of Hibiscus Prime when the communications bug in her ear chimed.

"E i ai sau valaauga ulufale."

Inez nearly jumped, forgetting she had it in. Then she sighed, and tapped the ear piece. "Can you repeat that?"

"Sie haben einen eingehenden Anruf." A call.

"Put it through."

"Ms. Stanton," a stern female voice said on the other end of the line.

"Are you from the Company?"

"Yes. You have a new job." Inez steered the patched up cargo hold away from her rig. She was using the virtual joysticks to control the pitch, velocity, yaw, and roll to make it line up. This station somehow didn't have automatic systems for that.

"Already? I know I've just aged ten years in the last week."

Silence. Somehow, even just by voice, it was very pointed.

"Alright, fine. What is it?"

"We're sending you the details in a secure packet. Please read the details this time. This is not a normal cargo run."

"So," Inez paused for a moment before asking the question, partly for emphasis, and partly because she was turning the cargo hold to match up with the docking ring, "why the call?"

"This job is very sensitive. It is important for the future of the Company. We just wanted to be sure that was something you were going to take seriously."

"Got it. No fuck-ups, no side trips. Just the cargo run."

"Colorful, but succinct. As much as we appreciate the dedication you showed at the waystation, that is exactly the sort of thing we do not want to have happen."

Inez squinted a little as the cargo hold's unloading side came into contact with the docking station's loading bays. She slapped the connection button and the controls went slack. "That makes eighteen thousand and two of us."

The call cut off. Inez's cargo of twenty four crates of inert biostock included one crate that was human biostock. Slaves, in other words. Typical Free Earth bullshit that she wouldn't have even known about if the rig hadn't been nearly destroyed by space debris.

Well, she may have another job, but she was still going to see what this station had in the way of food.

She was in the outer ring, looking through windows at her rig and the cargo hold. There were a number of automatons making their way around her, busily gathering and inspecting and ferrying. She sent a command to her rig to lock the entrance, and turned around the other way.

This station was quite a bit larger than Fang's Waystation was. It was serving as the gateway to the new settlement on the planet. This world had been terraformed over the last ten years, which was a long time (about as long as Inez had been driving a rig), but still not nearly as long as the two centuries it used to take.

They'd needed to figure out how to speed up the process thanks to the fact that the Hands of the Gods would sweep in on terraforming colonies and obliterate them without any warning. The Hands were about as alien as it was possible to be, by choice. Decades into a war with them, and as far as anyone knew, the Free Earth had never even collected a DNA sample from one. This led to lots of speculation that they were a malevolent artificial species, but Inez never believed that.

According to the brochures, each with the smiling face of the Colonial Affairs Secretary on the front, there were three million people across the planet, and more coming all the time. It was billed as a paradise, where the Free Earth citizens could live without the stress of doing any manual labor. It was a lie, of course. Anyone who knew the Free Earth knew that there were strata of "citizens", and then there were non-citizens, and below that, slaves.

She found her way to one of the tubes connecting the outer ring with ones closer to the center. There were ads on the walls, next to the permanent images of the Secretary, selling everything from temporary companionship to good old honest fucking. It seemed that some professions were always going to prosper. Not that she hadn't gone in for some honest fucking on occasion, but right now she was hungry.

At the next ring, Inez stopped at a wall display. "Directory," she said quietly. The display shifted from an outer view to a local view, complete with a flashing triangle: "You Are Here." She thumbed through the food offerings, finally settling on a promising looking Grpran place. The display helpfully showed her how to get there from here, and then was almost immediately replaced by a large penis.

This actually made Inez back up, which in turn made her bump into a woman who was walking along with a small child.

"I'm sorry," she said, and woman looked her up and down, said nothing, and continued walking along. The child turned back to look at Inez. She waved at him (she thought it was a boy, it was so hard to tell at that age), and he shyly smiled at her. Well, at least the kid wasn't an asshole. Yet.

"Right, off to get some gzzliphan." Zzrft had talked about missing gzzliphan a lot during the year on the ag planet, but it wouldn't tell her what it was. It probably thought she would think it was disgusting. Two years later, when she found herself at another station that served Grpran food, she ordered it without even checking the menu. The staff working there turned purple with surprise. Turned out, it wasn't on the menu, but they were happy to make it for someone from outside of their culture who knew what she wanted.

She imagined it would be much the same at this place. Grprans were often employed on space stations because of their ability to work for 70 hours straight, so it only made sense that they would bring their food along. Their home world was on the edge of the Orion arm towards the outward side, and until humans had discovered them they didn't have much interest in leaving.

The sign for the place was only thirty meters away, but it was much dimmer than the other signs all around it. She made her way inside, ducking through the doorway (Grprans were typically under a meter and a half tall). A host caught sight of her immediately.

"Welcome, welcome. Will you be dining alone today?"

"Looks like."

"We have our menu translated into Free Earth, if you would prefer."

"No, thanks, I'd just like some gzzliphan and a wheat beer."

"Wonderful, wonderful. Why don't you make yourself comfortable and we'll bring that right out."

Inez sat on one of the amorphous cushions that were scattered around the dimly lit room. A different Grpran came up to her with her beer. "Hello, I'm Krfit, I'll be your waiter today. Did you want any mraakin to start?"

"Why not?"

"Excellent. Enjoy your drink."

The Grpran wheat beer was not like a typical Earth wheat beer. They took the earth grain, added their own spices, and instead of a light, slightly hoppy brew, they came up with an intense (and highly alcoholic) drink. It burned a bit as it went down, but Inez relished it.

Krfit brought out six mraakin on a platter. They were small nibbles that appeared to be like stuffed mushrooms, except that the mushroom "caps" had legs. She took one and popped it in her mouth. The mraakin popped back, with more flavors bursting out of delicate spheres that melted as she ate. It was savory and (unsurprisingly) fishy, and she made a mental note that this may be her new favorite food.

As she finished the last morsel, a cart was wheeled out containing her main course. Gzzliphan is a native Grpran fish-like creature, and the traditional preparation has it butterflied, seared, and sauced with a peppery sea leaf-based concoction that had to be made fresh or it would be putrid. Several companies had tried bottling it, but no matter what they did, it would be horrible. Considering how much of a staple the leaf was to their cuisine and culture, there was certainly a large tank here filled with it.

If Inez believed in heaven, it would be these small moments.

The "fish", as much as it could be termed that, was more of a streamlined blob, with an exoskeleton but no internal bones. The meat that was seared had a sweetness to it, and the raw flesh by the outer bone was slightly bitter, but not unpleasantly so. She'd had so much to thank Zzrft for, and this was probably third on the list.

Her meal finished, she had the waiter put it on her rig's tab (she'd figure out the money later), and headed back to the outer docking ring.

● ▬ ▬ ▬ ▬▬▬▬▬ ▬ ▬ ▬ ıı((◉))ıı ▬ ▬ ▬ ▬▬▬▬▬ ▬ ▬ ▬ ●

The automatons were about halfway done getting the crates off the cargo hold. Inez didn't need to stay, the cargo hold was the property of the Company, and they'd be around to collect it. They'd probably junk it, considering the level of damage that had been done by the debris. She still kind of wanted to make sure that the one that was full of people (she wouldn't think of them as slaves, they deserved better) was at least safely delivered. But she had a job that was, based on the tone from the Company, urgent.

Inez unlocked the entrance to her rig and stepped through. She still wasn't used to how clean and not used it looked. The mechanotrons at the waystation had been thorough, and she was amazed at the change.

She made her way through her bunk (which used to be the storage room) and into the cab. She sat down, and looked over at Lui. Lui was a mechanotron that had grown attached to her after everything that went down at the waystation. Their AI wasn't especially advanced, but they were capable of developing loyalty.

(It turned out that humans trying to create intelligence would only ever create their own impression of what intelligence was, which meant it was inherently flawed and incapable of independent creativity. In the last couple centuries, developers focused instead on narrow but deep AI, creating very specialized intelligences that didn't have much knowledge outside their own fields, but were beyond experts within their fields.)

Lui was currently in box form. It stayed closed in that shape until it felt it was needed, but it was always on and aware.

She turned her seat toward the front-facing console, and piloted the rig away from the docking station. Once she was free of the station's influence, she turned toward the message from the Company. "The Tenth Great and Glorious Browns Company" had existed in one form or another for over 800 years. They were the Orion Arm's largest logistics organization, and who you turned to if you needed something to get from one place to another.

"IS:

"Your job is to collect German Bolivar, plus cargo, from Palestine and deliver him as quickly as possible to a meeting on Earth. You must personally hand him off to ensure his safe delivery.

"GM."

Earth? The Earth? The center of the Free Earth and all of its bullshit? Well, no wonder they didn't want to tell her until she'd already accepted the job. On the other hand, they hadn't actually given her a choice about it.

Palestine wasn't much better. It was another outer-edge world about 500 light years away, so that would take a couple days to get there. But it was disputed, and regularly in conflict with Free Earth forces, so depending on the current cease fire status, she might be flying into a war zone.

The person she was picking up was not a familiar name to her. There were more details in the job dossier, but not the sort of thing she was looking for. Was this a diplomatic mission? Was she picking up someone from the Palestinian side, or someone from the Earth side? Or neither?

It also didn't list the priority designation, but that was normal on most of her jobs. It was so rarely a high priority job that they usually forgot to fill it out.

She wasn't going to find out anything just sitting around, though. She added the coordinates that were attached to the message to the navigation system, and set the drive to 70%. This ship was so smooth now, she didn't even notice the transition.

Over the last couple of days, ever since leaving the waystation, she had told herself that she wasn't going to call Sara. Not doing it. There was someone else out there who could help her with the encrypted data she had copied off the Free Earth dreadnought's data core. Anyone else. Sara didn't need to be made a part of this.

Not that Sara had any loyalty to the Free Earth. Not long after Inez had left, Sara set off for the inner rim colonies. They were keeping to opposite ends of the Orion Arm, and the last she knew, Sara had put her inherited euan into buying a small automated mining concern, staying far away from people.

Not that she was keeping tabs. Maybe a bit.

Now, with more days to go before making the pickup, it was really hard to focus on doing anything else. She couldn't make any inquiries or searches on the subject of decryption without some major red flags popping up in the Free Earth's monitoring. She already thought she was being watched, but after the past week, it was now far more likely than before.

She could, however, check up on an ex, even an ex that was the daughter (legally) of a man she had killed in order to gain her freedom. It was a long story, and she didn't need to go over that again. She could check on other exes, as well, but that was hardly going to get her more than a couple of hours of looking.

She already knew Ihuoma was married, and Vicki, queen of disappearing, was probably a thousand feet below the surface of a planet looking at evidence of long dead civilizations. Diego could rot in prison, for all she cared. Zzrft was still working those ag planet stints, getting drunk and probably fucking anyone who was interesting. Poor Zzrft.

On the other hand, Sara was bright in her mind. Sparkling, in fact. She had sparks going off all around her and beyond that, fireworks and--

Inez snapped awake. Damn, that beer (and the five after it) must have been deceptively strong. She would need to make sure she left a good review for them.

The thing that woke her up was an incoming message.

"IS:

"Change of plans. Do not go to Palestine. Bolivar will charter a local ship and meet you outside of the system. Coordinates to follow.

"GM."

That still didn't give her a lot of information about who this guy was. On the other hand, if he's not with Free Earth, and she searched for information on him, chances are they would catch onto it. As much as she pretended otherwise, the Free Earth intelligence agencies were not stupid. Staying off their radar seemed like a good plan, overall.

She redirected the rig to the new coordinates, and wandered out to her bunk.

"Turn off the lights," she said.

"Yebo, nduna."

The Admiral's sneering face bore down on her, chasing her through the mansion. She wasn't allowed in the mansion, and he'd caught her sneaking in. He was blind drunk and ready to do a lot of damage in his anger.

Saw him reach for his sidearm, and before she knew what she was doing, she kneed him in the groin and grabbed it away from him.

"You little chicken shit," he growled, and slapped her across the face. "You fucking little bitch."

She'd been around this man's guns her entire life. She flipped off the safety, stuck the barrel under his chin. "Say that again," she snarled.

"Fucking c--" She pulled the trigger, and the Admiral's head flew off of his body. The infrasonic blaster was efficient and clean. His body didn't even bleed. She pushed it off of her, and looked around to see where the head had gone.

It was about three meters away, the eyes open. The mouth moved. "You'll never be worthy of her love."

Inez screamed, which woke her up. Fucking hell. That was not how it had actually gone down. She was sixteen and far less of a badass, not to mention that once she had shot him, his head stayed still. Far away from his body, but still.

That was the first time anyone had died at her hand. And she couldn't claim it was entirely self defense. She definitely wanted him dead. Given his treatment of her mother, not to mention his treatment of her before her mother had died, she felt it was completely understandable.

Sara understood. She had no love for the man, and she'd been raised by Inez's mother as much as by her own. But it was still a shock to Inez that she helped to vaporize the man's body after Inez panicked.

By the light coming in from the doorway, she could see the bare walls around the bunk. That was probably why she was having odd dreams. She usually had blankets all around, hanging from above, a bit of warmth in the coldness of space.

She could also feel the beginnings of a hangover, so she went out, into the corridor, and around to where her bunk used to be. It was a large closet that was more than big enough for her bed and some boxes, but the mechanotrons were going by the original ship specs when they fixed everything.

She saw the medical supplies box, and opened it. The supplies had apparently been restocked, so she took an anti-inflammatory pill and put it in her mouth. Then she grabbed a bottle of water and downed the entire liter.

She was thinking of Sara a lot the past week. And with Sara came all the shit that went down at the end. That had to be where the nightmare came from. That and probably the alcohol. She used to have those dreams a lot. Zzrft would wrap her in its tentacles and hold tight whenever it happened during that year on the ag planet.

She checked the time. Apparently, she'd been asleep for ten hours. That was quite a bit more than she had planned on, and from what she could tell, there were only a few hours left before the rendezvous.

She took a food bar out of the storage bin and ate it. Not nearly as good as her last meal, but it would help take the edge off the hangover.

On her way past, she peered through the cargo hold door. It was just space on the other side, but it was one of the few places she could actually get a look at the deep nothing out there. Eleven years since she'd first been in space, and it was still very strange. The stars didn't twinkle. They barely moved, even while she knew she was going far faster than the speed of light.

The lights were dimmed through the ship, so she turned to a wall panel (more of these were working now, as well) and turned them up. As much as the hangover made this a painful thing, it was better to rip the bandage off than to try and do it slowly. That's what she would keep telling herself.

●- - - - ━━━━━ - - — ιιι((◉))ιιι — - - ━━━━━ - - - ●

Three and a half hours later, Inez slapped her cards down on the table. "Gin."

Lui, across from her, laid its cards down. A display window popped up. "I will defeat you soon."

They had been playing since after she'd left the waystation, off and on, and the only part of the game that was getting better on Lui's part was the trash talking. "Ah, Lui. It's not gonna happen."

A chirp came from the cab, so Inez got up to check on it. They were approaching the spot for the meeting. Finally, something happening. Didn't she used to enjoy the long stretches of nothing?

Inez set the deceleration program, and they dropped out of faster than light speed. This spot was literally the middle of nowhere. It was fifty light years from any star systems, and thus perfect for some clandestine activity.

She was there first, clearly, as there were no other ships. However, within a few minutes, another ship--no, ships--had dropped to standard speeds and were coming to a stop. She could see why there were multiple ships. They were towing a small cargo hold that they were not built to carry along.

A ping came from one of the two ships. "Is this the Browns?"

"Yes," she replied, "I'm here to pick up Mr.--"

"Yes, yes," the other end said, cutting her off. "Open channels and all that. We're detaching from the cargo hold, and will back away from it until you are able to connect."

"Understood," she said, and cut the channel. This was less than ideal. She didn't know if Bolivar would be on the hold, or on one of the ships. It was all more cloak and dagger than a typical run for power converters.

She got the all clear for the cargo hold, and then got the command authorization from the unit. She had it use its positioning thrusters to turn it around and bring it down to the level where she was. The computer was able to plot the rest of it and within a few minutes, the seal connecting the two was complete.

Inez crossed out of the cab to the cargo hold door. Through the door's porthole, she could see the opposite door, which didn't have a window of any sort. She hauled the door open, and then opened the next door.

Laid out in front of her was a tall man, entombed in a personal stasis unit, in the middle of a personal cargo unit. He was completely inert.

2

This thing must have cost a fortune. Sending a large number of living beings inert was cost effective, due to the ability to cram as many as possible into as small a space as possible. That offset the cost of actually rendering them inert.

This Bolivar was put through the process all by himself. From what she had heard, it was not a terribly pleasant thing. You weren't frozen. Instead, your body's electrical activity was suppressed to a point where you were, for all intents and purposes, dead. Then, you were put into the chamber and surrounded with gasses to keep you preserved.

Then there was the cargo hold, if you could call it that. It looked more like a bare-bones hotel suite. There were several rooms, and clearly some luggage. She'd only ever had one of these on her rig once in the past.

It seemed that he was really running from something. There was a small data core next to the casket. She took it and crossed back over to the rig and to the cab. She took the data lead from the console and plugged it into the cube. It lit up and turned different colors, and then a display appeared in front of her.

It was a recording of the inert man. "Hello, courier. I know it's you, because the encryption on this data cube is specific to the Company."

He was dark, with hair going gray at the temples. He had a thick mustache, and appeared hale. He could be anywhere from 40 to 70 years old. Handsome, distinguished, with a joke playing behind his eyes. Inez sighed and rolled her eyes. "Politicians."

"I will need for you to take me to Earth. More to the point, I'll need for you to take me without having the Free Earthers scan or board your ship. The risk if I am caught will be catastrophic."

Delusions of grandeur. Money will make you think you're important, when really you're just a jackass in a nice suit.

"In addition to your usual payment and bonuses from the Browns, I am also authorizing one thousand euan to be transferred to you. You get half now, and you will get half when I have been safely delivered."

Well, maybe he wasn't that bad.

"I am to be revived once we are within five days of Earth. The instructions on how to do so are on this cube. I'm sure you have questions. They will have to wait."

Delusions, again. She had stopped caring who this guy was, but she would do everything in her power to make sure he got where he was going. A nice, clean, no-moral-quandary chance at paying off her rig sounded like just the thing she needed. So what if she had to go straight into the heart of everything she hated? This was going to be easy.

The display changed to a list of instructions. It also included the spot where he was to be dropped off. The spaceport in Oslo. She would have to take him off the rig at the docking port, and take a taxi (which she would not be controlling) to a spaceport (where she had never been) that was three fucking blocks from the Free Earth palace.

They didn't call it a palace. It went against their populist image. But that's what it was. Brother Lin and his merry band of assholes with their iron grip on all real power in the Orion Arm all holed up in a castle right in downtown Oslo.

Her mother had taught her about Oslo. It was one of the many things about the history of the Free Earth that she'd had drilled into her at a young age. Pamela Stanton had never been to Earth, and so far neither had Inez. But they had read books about it, about how it used to be, and how it was now.

Some places, like Oslo, Moscow, and Johannesburg, were shining cities on a hill, kept that way by the iron fists of the local law enforcement. Others, like Boston, San Francisco, Beijing, and Trinidad, were walled-off slums that were run like prisons. Some places were still on the map, but straight up didn't exist. London, for instance, which had been destroyed during one of several uprisings against the Free Earth.

So getting this guy in around the Free Earth's defenses and dropping him off right on their doorstep without them catching on? That sounded like the kind of fun she needed. Who needed a fucking vacation now?

"Me," she said under her breath. "Still me."

●----━━━━--— ιι((◉))ιι —--●━━━----●

No, this job was not going to be easy to pull off. She was going to need help. Inez was on her bunk, staring blankly up, not registering the room around her at all. She could only see one thing, and that was Sara. Sara's clear gray eyes. Her long dark hair down her back. Her milk and tea skin so soft under Inez's rough hands.

"Stop," she said, loudly. "That is not going to get you anywhere."

The images faded from her mind, but she had the twin sensations of tightness around her heart and warmth between her legs. Still, following the thought train that had gotten her there, she had to admit that as bad an idea as it was, it was the best idea she had.

She couldn't put it off any longer. She was going to have to send Sara a message. Worse, text-only just wasn't going to cut it, not if she was going to send the second message as well. Sara had given her an encoding scheme to use if she ever needed it, but it involved putting a text message into video noise.

She went to the cab and pulled out the physical keyboard. She typed up the message, the things she needed to ask, the things she needed confirmed. Asking for more direct help, if she even would or could. Inez read over the message a dozen times, wondering about the word choice, agonizing over what she was really asking.

Then, the hard part. Inez tied her hair back so it looked like she had a shower of fireworks over her head. Sara had never seen her with her hair grown out. The Admiral always insisted she shave it off if it ever got more than a few centimeters long.

Right, starting this conversation.

"Hey, Sara." She stopped recording. "Hey there, gorgeous." No. "Greetings human." What the fuck was that?

Inez held in a deep breath, let it out slowly.

"Hi, my always. I know it's been a long time. I'm sorry. I should have messaged you sooner. You know me, always in my head.

"I sure would love to see you. I've had—" she swallowed a lump that was forming in her throat. "I've had kind of a rough go of it lately. I miss you. You've always been my friend, and I need a friend now.

"And please, I hope you know that if you ever, ever need a friend, I will drop everything like an ear of corn straight off the grill to find you. But you haven't asked."

She could feel tears pooling in her eyes, which made her angry. This was not the time for tears.

"Which is fine. I would though. I would come running. Love you, Skitty."

She stopped the recording. Skitty, god, she hadn't thought about that nickname since her mom had died. Skitty was Sara, who found a kitten when the two of them were three years old, and managed to keep it a secret from everyone other than Inez. She wondered if Sara had taken the cat, named Beetle, with her when she left.

Inez had some new games to try out. She had sort of stolen them, sort of borrowed them, from the deceased crew of another Company ship, and she needed a distraction now. The message had been sent out, and all she could do now was wait.

There was a puzzle game that looked interesting. She plugged the lead into the data cube, and a display popped up in front of her. She started the game, looking for a list of items in a picture before time ran out. It was harder than she thought it was going to be, and she found herself running out of time.

"Come on, you can find a fucking spatula, brainiac." She spied it, and tapped it. The clock stopped, with .63 seconds left. Damn, that got the heart racing. She was then taken to the next scene, and did it all over again.

Sara's reply couldn't possibly get to her in less than a day. An entire day of obsessing over every ping to come from the cab's console. She might not survive the waves of anxiety that were crashing over her every few minutes. Sure, last week she was struggling to survive, but now she was in real peril.

The game beeped at her. She had run out of time on this one. The same scene appeared, but the list of objects was different. "Oh, that's not fair," she mumbled at the display. "Not fair at all."

She heard another beep, and the game disappeared completely. One of the things that the rig does is connect automatically to any control systems for items on the cargo hold. Usually this isn't important, as the cargo typically is uninteresting. However, the message on her display was extremely relevant to her now.

"Stasis pod malfunction. Activating occupant."

Shit, shit, shit. Inez leapt out of her chair and sprinted over to the cargo hold. She could see the dark-colored stasis gasses being pushed out by an oxygen-nitrogen mix. She knew that it would start resuscitating him in moments. Why did no one have working equipment? Even rich fucks like (she assumed) this guy weren't immune.

"Lui, get in here!"

The small robot trundled in behind her.

"Lui, can you fix this?"

It stopped, probably downloading the specs. It moved over to the machine, and plugged itself into a port on the side. A display popped up over its head. "Negative. Human occupant will perish if I stop now."

"Right. Can you make sure it wakes him up correctly? Don't want the golden goose to die before he pays me."

"Affirmative."

"How long?

"Five minutes."

Inez batted at the display to close it. She might need to talk to Sara about giving Lui a voice. It was easier than going through the rig closing all of the dialog windows. They would just hover there if she didn't do anything.

There were more beeps as things were progressing in releasing Bolivar from the pod. The tang of ozone as the electrical suppressors turned off and the flat line display above his head showed murmurs, and then true beats. The brain activity showed increases, progressing from coma to deep sleep to REM sleep and, finally, consciousness.

The coffin's lid began to rise, and the walls fell away. The man looked like he was just getting up from a short, refreshing nap as he sat up and swung his legs over the edge.

"I take it we are close to Earth," he said, by way of introduction.

"Not really, no."

"What?" This clearly surprised him. He probably wasn't used to traveling as a package.

"Your pod had a malfunction, and the only way to save your life was to wake you up. Lui?"

The mechanotron disconnected and rolled in front of them. A window popped up in front of the man, but Inez couldn't read it. Even if she could make out the words from where she was, it was probably technical jargon that wouldn't make a bit of sense.

"Hmm. I see." Inez could not place the man's accent. "Well, we shall persevere. How far out are we?"

"Well, I only picked you up about ten hours ago. It was uneventful until your pod failed."

"And how many days until we reach Earth?"

"Probably about ten. We shouldn't need to stop anywhere prior to going in, but I'm still working on that plan. You should feel free to make yourself at home. Come on, Lui."

Inez left the cargo hold with the mechanotron on her heels. Having someone else here was not going to make planning easy, even if he was the package.

●■■■━━━━━━ ■■ ━ ııı((⦿))ıı ━ ■■ ━━━━━━ ■■■■ ●

For the most part, the difficulty in getting through to the Earth was going to be masking her ship's identity. She was fairly sure that Colonel Hynes was enough of an asshole to have the entire Free Earth fleet keep tabs on her. There was also the fact that German Bolivar was a wanted man. (She had finally done some limited research on him. He was a strategist for hire, working with anti-Free Earth factions all over the Orion Arm. His ability to get in and out without being noticed was one of his trademarks.)

Beyond disguising the ship, she was going to have to disguise herself, and Bolivar, in order to get from the ship to a taxi so she could finish the delivery. That meant fake ID implants, and biometric changes. The first one was reasonably easy. Inez had removed her ID implant long before, and she figured that Bolivar probably would have as well, so it was just a matter of mimicking an implant without actually attaching it to the bone.

The second part, it was literally impossible to fool the biometric readers that would be installed at all ends of the trip within the Earth's system. She was going to need to ask Sara about that as well.

Inez was writing these things down on a napkin. She didn't want any digital trace that could be stolen from her computer. She didn't even say anything out loud. She trusted Lui, but didn't necessarily trust anyone not to misuse the automaton.

Perhaps she should talk to Sara about making sure its security was higher quality than a typical mechanotron. (And perhaps so much of this plan shouldn't rely on Sara, who hadn't even responded to her message. Yet. It had only been a few hours. That probably wasn't even enough time for the message to reach her, let alone for her to record and encode a response.)

"Pardon," she heard from across the room and nearly fell out of her bunk. "Sorry, I don't mean to intrude, but I noticed you don't have cooking facilities on your ship."

"Um, no. No, it's a fairly basic setup. I eat a lot of meal bars."

"I would expect. I asked your ship's computer, but it seems to speak in Swahili?"

"Only sometimes. The translation matrix got fucked up a little while ago, so you never know what it's going to come out with."

"Interesting. Anyway, I have a full cooker in my suite, and making a meal helps me relax. Do you have any objections?"

"I have never objected to food in my life," she said with a smile. "Especially when someone is making me food."

"Excellent. I'll get to it, then."

The tall, handsome, aging politician-slash-freedom fighter offering to make her food was not something she had ever expected. Even if he was bad at it, the prospect of real food on this trip was amazing.

Soon, the entire rig was filled with the scents of garlic and onion, ginger, cumin, and lamb. Inez rummaged through her storage closet to find where her beer had disappeared to. This was definitely going to be a meal to enjoy. Planning getting to Earth could wait.

●▪▪▪▪━━━━━ ▪▪ ━ ıı((◉))ıı ━ ▪▪ ━━━━━ ▪▪▪▪●

The meal, a thick lamb stew served over rice (Bolivar called it "seco de Cordero"), was warming Inez from her stomach out to her toes. She finished a fourth bottle of beer (she was going to need to stock up the next time she was able to) and the combination of food drunk and drunk drunk was making her sleepy.

"So let me get this straight, you and this General—"

"Sexy General," Bolivar interjected.

"Right. Sexy General. You were fucking, timed to—"

"Exactly when the rebels attacked." He smiled, finishing his own beer. "Sometimes you must sacrifice for the greater good."

"Sacrifice. Fuck that. You just wanted to know where she hid all her guns."

"And I found them."

"She must have been hard up, because you are not that charming."

He touched his chest above his heart. "Oh, you wound me."

"I could."

3

Woken up again by incessant beeping. Did no one have any respect for an almighty hangover?

Inez was naked, and this wasn't her bunk. Oh, son of a bitch.

Bolivar was also very naked, and sleeping very soundly. She whipped the covers off and got out of his bed, collected her jumpsuit and underclothes, and made her way to the cab.

"Dammit, stop that noise."

The noise stopped, and was immediately replaced by a louder silence. She wrestled her way back into her clothes, and then focused on the display. Finally. Sara.

She started to mess with her hair, and then remembered that it wasn't going to be a live call. She started the play back.

At first, she wasn't sure it was Sara. Her skin was sallow, and she hadn't been eating. And her hair, gods. It looked like she'd hacked it off with a knife. She was heavy lidded. She was back taking the medication, which meant it was getting worse.

"Hey, little bee. It's good to see you. You look good. I'm so glad you called."

She really sounded glad. Oh, what was going on with her?

"You definitely seem to have a life of adventure going on. You and your rig, alone against the galaxy. A romantic, like always."

There was a trace of the old smile. Just a trace, over a lot of pain. Real, physical pain.

"I'm fine," she lied. "You know me, it's all fun and games." She coughed, and held a cloth to her mouth. She pulled it away and Inez was sure that she saw blood.

"Anyway, I have to run. Busy, busy." The video cut out there. Then the rest of the message came in:

"Little bee,

"Dammit, it really is good to see you. I don't know what you've gotten yourself into, but it doesn't matter. You are going into the heart of the Free Earth, and based on what you said about the data core, they won't be done with you. I need you to be safe. I need you alive.

"I'm attaching a new cypher that will let us talk openly over video. I still recommend making sure that your passenger isn't around to hear. But it will be good to talk.

"I'm close enough to Earth that we'll be able to talk in near real time. No, don't come looking for me. I'm fine.

"I love you, monster. Always."

The pet names hurt most. Little bee was what her mother called her when the two were very young, because she was always buzzing around. Sara was "princess", and was meant endearingly. Her mother had loved Sara like her own daughter.

"Monster" was a different matter. It was tinged a bit with anger at the Admiral. He had forbidden Sara from spending time with "that mossheaded monster." When Sara told her, Inez laughed, hard. They were 14 at the time, and Inez hated the man more than any other person. Sara was aghast at first, but then started laughing too.

Now, it just made Inez want to cry. This whole thing. She wished she hadn't involved Sara. Whatever was going on with her, she didn't need to be dealing with Inez on top of it all.

She zipped up her jumpsuit and settled back into her pilot's chair. She was going to have to respond. Not responding would just worry her. But just, not yet.

●- - - ━━━━━ - - ━ ıı((◉))ıı ━ - - ━━━━━ - - -●

Bolivar seemed to be keeping his distance from Inez. Whether that was due to some sort of embarrassment, or respect, or if he was just working on his own plans, she didn't know, and wasn't overly interested to find out.

A little interested.

Sara hadn't just sent her a new encryption scheme. She'd sent the current arrangement of the security forces in the Sol system. The first that she would need to get past was the Plutonic ring. It wasn't actually a ring, but a series of satellites orbiting the sun half an AU within the orbit of Pluto. Her rig would identify itself to these satellites, which would then signal the fleet to come in and blow her to smithereens.

Or just board the rig and arrest her cargo. It was a fifty/fifty shot, she figured.

She had to look like a normal Company ship to them, which meant reprogramming the transponder. Sara could probably whip something up to take care of that. The same fake out would work on the Jovian and Martian rings. But that's where the computers talking to computers would stop. When she came into Earth orbit, there would be a visual inspection. There would be face to face calls. They would need to get onto the docking station, get a taxi down to the surface, and somehow get all the way to his rendezvous point without being picked up.

The Free Earth controlled the system (as with many of the surrounding systems and colonies) like an abusive lover, with constant surveillance, threats of violence, actual violence (carried out by the military and state police), negging, and effusive praise of actions that showed subservience. Turning that from a liability to an advantage was the key.

They were going to need convincing disguises. With the right upgrades and supplies, Lui could probably make uniforms for them. They would need a fabricator. Wigs might also be useful.

She needed to get to a public terminal. She couldn't look these things up from the ship, or they would definitely be on to her. She was going to need to find a waystation with a lot of traffic, somewhere the Free Earth wasn't going to be looking for her, but wasn't deserted like Fang's had been.

She pulled up the star charts and looked for anywhere that would fit the bill. Beehive Cluster would be on the way, how busy was it? Thirty million passing through each year.

That had some promise. It's pretty close to Earth, though. What sort of presence would Free Earth have there? This was harder to find out, since waystations didn't typically advertise those figures.

It seemed like the best option, either way, so she had the rig change course.

They were about four days out, so lots of time to figure out next steps. For one thing, they weren't going to be able to get far with bad disguises. But also, they needed to change up things like their resting heart rate and blink rate. These were the sorts of things that made it difficult for wanted people to escape when they went deep inside.

It was far more than height and weight. The computers that analysts in the security division relied on had access to thousands of hours of recordings of everyone who was ever under the control or even in the space of the Free Earth. Inez never liked being watched. She had Lui make sure that there were no surveillance bots within the rig.

The Free Earth assholes that had access to her rig at Fang's waystation had, in fact, put some bugs in the cab, but Lui put them out the airlock.

The Company used to have recorders on the rig as well, but there was no sign of those at this point.

Inez heard some movement going on in Bolivar's room, and then started to smell cooking. Compared to the previous week (year? decade?), she was going to be well fed, and this was something she was going to try (probably fail) not to get used to.

●•••— •••— ɪɪ(((◉)))ɪɪ — •••— •••●

After they ate (this time, no sex resulted; Bolivar was very kind to not bring it up), Inez went back into the cab. She'd put it off long enough.

She had the computer read in the new cypher, and sent a ping to Sara, letting her know that she was on. There was a long wait, and it felt like it was so much worse than if she'd been right there. After the first bit, probably about 20 minutes, she went back to her game finding things in pictures just to get her mind off of it. She'd play all night to avoid missing Sara's call.

An hour and a half deep into looking for hypodermic needles (she wasn't even sure what that meant) and witches' brooms, the response finally came. She opened up the channel.

No, this was worse. The punch in the gut of seeing her, and seeing her in this state, this was far worse than waiting.

"Oh, Bee," Sara said, clearly noticing the stricken look her utter lack of poker face let through. She actually looked worse than she had in that earlier call.

"Gods, Sara. Is it the Gladwell's?"

"I've been worse. It's really good to see you." The only color on Sara's face were the dark circles under her eyes. She was so pale, no that's not right. She was wan. Inez had to reach into archaic words to make sense. Changing the subject.

"So, I found out something. The Admiral isn't my sperm donor."

Sara's eyes went wide. "You mean neither of us carry on his genes? That's a relief."

"Well, I don't think much of the genes I am carrying. Did you know one of his proteges, Abram Hynes?"

"No, but he didn't really have me around them."

"He's a real prick. He thinks he and Pamela had a great love. Kinda makes me want to puke thinking about it."

"Oh, don't bring up vomit," she said, turning a little green.

"Dammit, Sara. Why didn't you tell me things had gotten bad?"

"I could ask you the same thing."

"Me? Things were fine until last week."

"Your ship was nearly destroyed, and you along with it."

"But it wasn't. And you couldn't have done anything about it while it was happening."

"There more to it, though. I know you, bee."

Inez could feel tears welling up, and dammit, she was going to be stronger than this. "They were slaves!" she cried out, without even knowing it was coming. "My cargo, there were a few million head of livestock, and eighteen thousand slaves. They were all inert, in cargo containers, like they were less than animals." Inez couldn't even look at Sara. "And I delivered them. Because that's what I do."

"Oh, Inez," Sara said. She wasn't angry, she wasn't disappointed, she was just Sara. It was like how she reacted when Inez killed the Admiral. This was just a part of the girl she loved, and nothing could shake that. And for Inez, that was so much worse.

"No, I should have done something. I should have freed them, lost the cargo, run away! I should have--"

"Gotten yourself killed? Stayed on the run for the rest of your life? I know your contract with the Browns, bee. Losing cargo would have resulted in severe reprimands. You wouldn't have ever been free, and you know that those people would have been recaptured, and probably killed."

"How do you know--"

"I haven't spent the past ten years breaking into network systems without making sure my little monster was okay. I know we can't be together. But I love you, and that will never change."

The tears were impossible to stop now. "I don't," she started. "Oh, gods. Why?"

"I have never had cause not to believe in you."

Inez pulled herself together. It took a few minutes, but Sara didn't feel the need to fill the silence.

"What the hell are you doing, anyway?"

"I am basically bringing down the fascists from the inside."

"What the fuck are fascists?"

"Ancient Earth history. I'll send you a book or two on it. They hate anything they can't control, and depend on people being happy with things working for them personally, and even if they aren't working, that some common internal enemy has it worse."

"Well that's fucked up when you put it that way."

"Yes, indeed."

"And you're safe?"

"It's only my genes that are going to take me down. But not for a while yet."

"You look like hell, Skitty." She didn't mean to say it, but there it was.

"It looks worse that it is. The lambaprexin helps."

"What do you need?"

"I need you safe. So tell me what you need for your heist."

Inez laughed in spite of herself. "It's not a heist. It's the opposite of a heist."

"Disguises, right? Biometrics? Changing the ship's transponder?"

"My mechanotron can take care of a lot of that."

"But I'm better at it. I'm sending you the materials list and plans for a fabricator to use. You'll need a facilitator to get that, probably. Also, I have a firmware upgrade for your robot."

"Its name is Lui."

"I'm glad you have a friend with you now."

Inez was about to protest that characterization, but after a minute, she had to admit it was apt. "They're apparently very loyal. It's terrible at Gin, though."

"You and that game. I don't think that's Lui's fault. You always beat me, too."

"I don't want to stop talking to you."

"I know. I want to run to you right now. I can't. And not just because my legs are misbehaving."

The pit in Inez's stomach dropped. That was a progression in the disease. That was not things being better on the medication. And she knew, now. That was her way of letting Inez know that she wasn't going to be around forever.

"I will come to you when this is all over. Wherever you are, it doesn't matter. I will come to you."

"I love you, Bee." The channel cut off. Inez had trouble defining what her feelings were at this moment. She stood up, her fist already balled, and she just let it fly.

It hit Bolivar on the chin.

"Whoa, now," the older man said.

"Oh, fuck. Shit, fuck. I'm sorry, I didn't know you were there."

"It's not the first punch I've taken, dear." She'd usually bristle at being called "dear", but something in his voice told her it was actual endearment and not condescension. "I am sorry, I overheard some of your conversation."

"It's nothing. It won't get in the way of getting you to Earth." She wiped the tears off her face, not able to meet his gaze.

"I wasn't worried about that. Your friend, you didn't know how sick she was?"

She didn't want to have this conversation. She didn't want to think about it. She wanted to get drunk again, but they were dangerously low on alcohol.

"It's Gladwell's." Bolivar's face showed he didn't know the disease. "It's a genetically passed neuro-degenerative disorder that is eventually going to kill her. It sort of comes and goes, which is fucking maddening. She had an attack when she was 11 that almost killed her, but she bounced back and has been well for--" She stopped. "I guess I don't know how long she went without an attack. I haven't talked to her in years."

"Why not?"

"It hurt too much. It would shut me down if I thought about her. And then, it was just such a long time."

"You grew up together?"

"Her father owned me. And when I was sixteen, I killed him. And thanks to Sara, I'm still alive and not vaporized."

"But?" His eyes were soft, but she couldn't look at them still.

"But we were in love, and I wondered if she would have freed a slave she wasn't in love with. Fuck, why am I telling you this?"

"It sounds like you need more friends."

"I get by okay."

"You don't. I'm nearly twice your age, and I still don't know a way to survive life, especially a difficult life, without friends."

"Dammit," she said, softly. "Was there something you were coming in to tell me, or ask?"

"When we reach the Beehive cluster, there are some areas that you will want to avoid on your way into the station. I have some recent intelligence from there."

"Is it going to be safe for us to go there?"

"Safe is relative in my line of work. But we should be able to get what we need and get back out without being detected."

The console beeped. Inez turned back to it. "It looks like Sara's already got what we need to reprogram the transponder."

"Was she always a hacker?"

"I'm not sure what that term is, but at a guess, I'd say yes. She's been able to manipulate computer systems for a long time. I never had any talent for it, but then, I wasn't allowed to touch computers very much."

"I'm going to retire for the evening, dear. I shall see you tomorrow."

The Admiral was on top of her. He was taking her head in both hands and pushing her to the marble floor. She knew what was coming but she couldn't stop it. They rolled around, him trying to get a grip on her neck. "She's not your daughter," she spat at him, and then she actually spat at him.

He stopped trying to strangle her and back slapped her instead. Her head whipped back and hit the marble again. She kneed him in the groin and he wailed in pain. "You fucking bitch."

She reached for his sidearm, but it wasn't there. It's always there. Where the fuck was it?

She spotted it across the hall. She used all of her weight to push the man off her and darted to the pistol. He regained his stance and leapt at her back, pushing her past the gun and into the wall.

"You think you can fuck my daughter and I have no say in it?"

She whipped her head back and caught him on the bridge of the nose. She definitely heard it break, and he let go for just a moment.

She used that moment to reach the pistol and shot him in the head. She felt the gun shoot, she knew her aim was on, and his head was still there.

Sara came up behind and took his head off with a sword. But not Sara as she was then, Sara as she is now.

"Wake up, little monster."

Inez sat straight up in bed. Her heart was racing and there was a sheen of sweat on her skin. Well, sleep was fun while it lasted.

4

Inez put down her hand. "Gin, buddy."

Lui set its cards down and showed her a short video of a girl rolling her eyes.

"Another round?" Lui backed away. "I guess not. Alright, back to the wall."

Sara had sent along the upgrades to Lui's security, but she said she was not going to be able to give the mechanotron a voice. That was hardware, not software, apparently. At any rate, Lui was now able to be a part of the planning. Right now, its part in the planning was projecting the plan onto the wall.

The wall was split into four parts. The top left was Materials, the top right was People (four, including Sara and Lui). Bottom left had the individual steps, while the bottom right had the obstacles listed for each step. The bottom right was almost entirely red with writing.

They were still a day out from Beehive, and she didn't actually have a set plan of what they needed to get from there. She checked her account, and the 500 euan that Bolivar had promised was there, so materials (especially the expensive long-chain polymers to make clothes for the disguises) could be procured. Those would be available in shops on the station on the off chance their facilitator couldn't provide them.

The fabricator would have to be a small one, and it would not be cheap. They were going to need an agent to help them get it because it wasn't the sort of thing that individuals would just pick up on a whim. And to make sure they didn't get picked out, the agent would need to be sympathetic to Bolivar's faction.

"Hey, Bolivar," she called, and momentarily he popped his head into the room. "Do you know any procurement agents who can help us get a small, professional fabricator? That's not exactly something we can just waltz in and ask for."

"I assume you mean, someone who is not going to report us to the enemy?"

"Assume what you--I mean, yes." It was still hard to remember that not only could she trust him, he was trusting in her. He was also the entire reason she was doing this, so being snide wasn't really going to help anyone. That's a tough one to turn off.

"Let me check my resources. We may need to go with a graycoat, if a whitecoat can't be found."

"That would make things a little dicier. Let me know what you can find."

Inez had to admit that this was feeling a bit heist-like. She had read a number of old novels about teams of experts breaking into the impenetrable to obtain the most valuable, and they were fun, but they never felt terribly realistic to her.

Once they were away from Beehive, then the real obstacles started to mount. Lui would be making the disguises, and Sara should be done breaking into Free Earth security to change their biometric records. Not a lot, but enough to throw off detection.

When they were on the docking station (it would have to be station B12-Omega, that was the one geostationary over Oslo), they needed to very quickly get a taxi to the surface. The problem was, there was truly no such thing as getting a quick taxi. There were horror stories of families living on B12-Omega for months before managing to get down planetside.

(One of the books about fascism that Sara had sent her referred to one of the rulers having made the trains run on time. It wasn't actually true, just a wistfulness for the totalitarian thugs that kept things orderly. As long as you were in the favored demographic, at least.)

They were going to need to jump the line, and that wasn't an exploit Sara could do remotely. She was going to have to give Inez something she could run on the station.

A small data core could give her some level of access, but it would need to be extremely secure for that. Otherwise as soon as she plugged in, it would be raining Free Earth thugs.

The obstacles were growing. Bolivar wasn't even sure, exactly, what building the meeting would be in (or, more likely, under). He would find out by the time they got there, but it still made planning that much harder.

And all the while, they would be under surveillance. Every single step off this ship would be watched. Which meant, sleight of hand, obscuring, blocking. But Inez had an idea about that.

"I don't get it," Sara said, looking at a hologram of a personal comms system. It was designed to go on the wrist and have the same range as a ship's communications array.

"I was reading one of those old spy novels you sent." Sara always had great taste in bad novels. "One of the things that aircraft and ships could do to make themselves harder to spot was to throw out interference to jam the signals that were looking for them. If we got a couple of these, do you think you could help me turn them into jammers?"

"Maybe? What signals are you looking to jam?"

"Video feeds, audio, biometrics, anything that might identify us. I want you to make us invisible. Obviously, not physically, but invisible to all of their sensors."

Inez could see that Sara was thinking about it now. "Video sensors tend to be in the high bands, but biometric scanners are low band. This is going to take some very precise tuning, if it's possible."

"Thanks."

"It's still a big 'if', so you'll need a backup in case this doesn't work."

"It'll work. I have faith."

Sara pulled up schematics on the device. "You're sure you can get these at Beehive?"

"Or something very similar."

"Alright. Has Bolivar heard from his agent?"

"Not yet. He has assured me that he has someone who will take care of it, but I won't trust them until we're in the clear."

"Do you trust German?"

"Kind of. I mean, I trust that he wants to survive this, so he's not going to fuck me over."

"That's not what I asked, Inez."

"I know what you asked. And, I do? I don't know. All this crazy shit going on. Two weeks ago, I was just an anonymous cargoist. Now? Suddenly I'm on the Free Earth's radar, and the Company is giving me special assignments. And no, I don't trust the Company."

"The Browns have existed in one form or another since--"

"All the more reason not to trust them. How do they endure for centuries of changing political fuckery and still have more business than the Gods?"

"Money will grant you a certain immunity. I've found that out." She chuckled, but that turned into a cough. She turned off the sound, but Inez could still see her having trouble. She watched her type something out, which then appeared on the screen. "Logging off so medics don't stumble on it." And then she was gone.

Inez was left with a stabbing worry punching out through her chest.

Her eyes felt puffy, and she was sure they were cherry red, but better to just deal with it. She turned the corner into Bolivar's cabin, and saw him sitting at a low table across from Lui. They weren't playing gin, but she couldn't quite tell what card game they were playing. It was definitely going better for Lui than gin did, because there was a short video of someone pointing and laughing on a loop hanging in front of the passenger.

"Good for you, Lui," she said, and Lui gave her a little wave. "What are you teaching my mechanotron, Bolivar?"

"Golpeado. It's similar to your gin, but Lui seems to be a bit better at it."

"Well, you done good, Lui, but it's not nice to trash talk a guest."

A window popped up, replacing the video, that just said, "Sorry."

Bolivar had clearly seen that she wasn't in a fit state, but he wasn't going to mention it if she didn't. She wasn't sure if that was kindness or chivalry, but she'd take it right now.

"Have you heard back from your friend?"

"I don't know that I'd call Ingmar a friend. But he's friendly to the cause. He's not able to be our agent there, but he's let me know of another."

"Graycoat?"

"Graycoat. Name is Foster Rios. I've been checking up on him. He's certainly got no love for the Free Earth. He's also shown no indication of having his own agenda, other than making money for himself. And luckily, I have money."

"How?" Inez asked before she could stop herself. "How does a revolutionary for hire have the kind of euan lying around to pay both the Company and me individually an unbelievable amount?"

"I wasn't always a revolutionary for hire, as you say. Once, I was a businessman, and then a politician. These are both lucrative fields, and I was quite successful, but before that, I was already quite wealthy. I was born into wealth I didn't deserve."

"Okay, that explains the money, I guess. Those credentials don't generally lead to your current line of work."

"I was the mayor of a city, Nueva Lima, and a member of the Senate for the colony as a whole. We voted, unanimously, to secede from the Free Earth. This was over thirty years ago, and Brother Xavier wasn't quite as convinced of his inevitability as Brother Lin. When Lin succeeded, he started by bringing the colonies back into the fold, either by persuasion, or by force.

"I was in the capital doing work when they hit. Nueva Lima was wiped from the face of the planet. My family, well, I am all that I have now. Our people were firm, but could never stand against a military like that, and so after an emergency session, the surrender was approved.

"I had no reason to stay after that. Some of my colleagues wanted to start fighting a guerrilla war, but we soon realized that with our current lack of standing, it would only end up hurting our own people. And so I went out to the other colonies to work, studying how to be successful at revolution, hoping to one day bring it back home.

"Alas, that day won't come. Free Earth destroyed my home, using it to test radiation weapons that ran out of control."

"I think I encountered some of those recently."

"They are horrible. And they are too powerful. They are a bomb hurled at a gnat. They may kill the gnat, but also anything else that gets in its way."

"So, Rios. He'll be able to get us in on a fabricator?"

"I've already put out a request, text only, and he will meet you at the station."

"And he's not going to fuck us over." This was more statement than question, and said more to reassure herself than to verify it with Bolivar.

"He will know that to do so would be unwise."

"I really hate involving other people. It's already four of us. How many more will we need?"

"That depends on our cover once we get to B12-Omega."

A noise startled Inez then. She looked over, and Lui was shuffling the cards. "I'll let you get back to it, then."

Dammit, that was another thing to add to the obstacles side. They didn't just need disguises, they would need a cover story, which might mean people to confirm their cover story. But it also needed to be something that wasn't going to draw attention to them.

They wouldn't be able to sneak in as Free Earth enlisted military, since they wouldn't have the right ident chips. Business conducted on Earth was tightly controlled, so being businesspeople probably wouldn't work, either. But just standard earth citizens were generally not afforded permission to go down to the surface. Most maintenance of Earth buildings was done by automaton, so pretending to be the cleaning crew (like in spy novels) was also not going to work.

Bot maintenance, though. There's a thought. A lot of the maintenance on automatons was done by other automatons. However, there were things that they couldn't fix, and so humans needed to be involved. With the right credentials, they would be able to move about freely, and it would give them an excuse to bring Lui along. It could be very helpful for getting where they needed to go.

She was happy she hadn't yet painted flames on its sides like she wanted to.

So what would they need to pull this off? The typical bot maintenance staff would have augmentations built right into their skulls. Obviously, that was out of the question, but they would be able to manage it with the right prosthetics.

Prosthetics would mean a supply of skyn, the artificial skin substance that was always at the edges of the augmentations. It had a look that was almost-but-not-quite skin-like, and nearly impossible to fake.

They were also going to need ident chips. They would be able to use them without having them implanted, just taped around their forearms. Unlike a slave's ident chip, which was implanted under the sternum, a worker's chip was attached to the ulna. A long sleeve maintenance uniform would be more than enough to cover that up. She wrote all of these things down to send to Sara.

It had been hours since that last call. She knew when Sara had an attack in the past, it could be over quickly or take three or four days under heavy sedation. And wherever she was (Inez still hadn't gotten that out of her), she was concerned about people spying on her. She was paranoid when they were younger, but that was because of the

Admiral. This, all of this, there was more than the Gladwell's going on.

As far as Inez knew, Sara still owned the mine, and she had been running it herself. It was about as far from the gilded world of her childhood as it was possible to get. But if she had to hazard a guess, Sara was on a science station, and if she was near Earth, that was a short list of possibilities.

They would be in the Beehive cluster in less than a day. It was a stellar neighborhood about 600 light years from Earth, filled with all kinds of stars, including red giants and white dwarfs, not to mention a number of Sol-like stars. The station, also just known as Beehive, orbited one of these smaller stars that only had a wide asteroid field and no planets. It was initially set up to take care of mining operations (there were lots of heavy metals and other useful minerals in the asteroids), but soon it became a hub for all sorts of trade.

Once they had entered the cluster, it would take about half a day to maneuver around the various stars, and then the asteroids, to get to the station. Assuming nothing went wrong, a bit under forty hours until they had to make the first part work.

Bolivar could have passed as a business man. He had normal business clothes and a lot of charm. Inez, on the other hand, pretty much only owned jumpsuits at this point. They were comfortable, had lots of pockets, and required no thought.

Maybe she would have to play his personal pilot. Chauffeur. Employee. This was not something she relished. She had employers, of course, but they were mostly nameless and faceless Company people and it was easy to go on like they weren't in charge of her. Having an "employer" this close was a little too much like having an owner for her comfort.

"He is not my employer and I am getting paid." Saying it out loud, it sounded ludicrous, which helped dull the edge.

Time for a break. She fired up the hidden object game again. Let her brain work on this whole thing on its own, without any input from her conscious mind. That was a thing, right?

Bolivar poked his head into the cab and coughed softly. Inez was not startled (maybe a little startled), and glared at the door where he stood.

"I've heard back from Rios. He'll take the job and is currently working to source a fabricator. I figured we'd spring anything else on him when we get there."

"What's his rate?"

"Thirty. But don't worry, that's on my end."

"Who's worried?" Inez asked, then, "About money, I mean. This whole plan could go ass up at any point. It's entirely choke points. Even the choke points have choke points. Every part of this could go wrong, and then it's improvisation city, three blocks from the palace. Oh, and Brother Lin is actually going to be there, so there's extra security."

"Yes, that's actually part of why I'm going there now."

"You know, I don't want to know that part of it. In fact, the less I know about what you're doing after I drop you off, the better."

"Fair enough. There's a lot of parts to it, which is why we won't know exactly where to go in Oslo until we get there. On the plus side, Oslo has some fantastic cafes and a counter-culture nightclub scene, in case you were looking for something to do."

"Been reading the brochures?"

"I lived there, for a time. Hidden, but working. Lin was still new and didn't have his support as shored up as he would have wanted, so I could do that. I knew a number of the members of his inner circle, though they had no idea just who I was. Some of them are still close to the man."

Inez cradled her forehead in her hand. "In other words, there are people close to the leader of the Free Earth who might recognize you, and we are walking straight the fuck towards them." She sighed. "Swell."

"It's not as bad as all that."

"You have a strange sense of what's good and bad, my man."

"They wouldn't want to let on that they know me. Lin would definitely have them shot, if he didn't do it himself."

Inez was fighting off a headache now, one that wasn't alcohol related. "Godsdammit, I don't know if this plan will work to begin with, and now you throw this in? That settles it. You have to shave off your mustache."

5

Beehive Station was hexagonal, but Inez didn't know if that was due to thematic planning or some other design imperative. She'd parked the rig at the Company's berth (there was only one other Company ship there), and then she disembarked alone. This was going to be a solo mission after all.

She had her duffel strapped to her back, and the ship's ear-piece that would let her stay in contact with Bolivar. She knocked on the door to the Company's office, opened it and poked her head in.

"We didn't have you scheduled to come in," was the response from the bored looking man seated behind an extremely messy desk.

"I didn't either, but supplies aren't going to buy themselves."

"Hmm," he said, but didn't press. "You have an L1 delivery right now, don't you?"

"I'm still well within the delivery time frame."

"Browns HQ marked you as 'No questions asked,' so I won't." Except you are, Inez thought. "They usually give those to people who are already prepared."

"I just need to get on. Yes, it's an L1, and if you aren't going to help me, they will know who kept me off my schedule," she read the nameplate on the desk, "Sven."

"No need to get hostile," he said, placating then. "We don't get a lot of L1s going through here."

"No, no, I'm sorry. We didn't get off on the right footing. And, frankly, since this is an L1, I need you to do me a favor."

His eyebrows, which were already arch, raised even further. "What is it?"

"I need you to get me into the station under a different name."

It took some convincing (and ten euan) to get Sven to do it, but Company bureaucrats were nothing if not bribable. Inez got a station passport under the name Gidget Perez, which was the name Bolivar had provided Rios for the contact. It was just ludicrous enough to be believable.

She actually had no idea that they'd designated this mission an L1. It hadn't even occurred to her, and the designation on the job detail had been blank. L1 meant that she could use resources she didn't even know about. There was supposed to be special training for L1 cargoists, and the highest training Inez had done was T5. The only level above L1 was L0, and that was practically a myth. Based on cargoist rumors, the last L0 was 70 years ago(they were the "Ninth Brown Regiment" at that time), and did not go well.

Inez ducked into a restroom that was right outside the Company berth. It was deserted, like much of this part of the station. She pulled a set of business clothes out of the duffel. They were Bolivar's, but Lui had altered them to fit her (thanks to Sara's tailoring program). The trend in business clothes over the last decade had been largely the same for men and women: garish clashing colors that made Inez's eyes burn and fabrics that were 100% polymerized glass, and skin tight. Comfort was not part of the program.

Inez shrugged on the suit, kind of amazed at the elasticity the material had, and stuffed her jumpsuit and underclothes into the duffel. Gidget Perez, Gigi to her friends, emerged from the restroom, trying to look like she owned the place.

Her ear-piece chirped. "What is it?" she said under her breath.

Bolivar's voice came through more loudly than she had expected. "We've been able to get into the public video surveillance feed." He paused a moment as the oxymoron washed over them both. "Anyway, we were the only ones paying attention to the restroom."

"Yay? I hate this suit. This is the opposite of stealthy."

"You'll say otherwise when you get to the commerce sector."

"My entire ass is hanging out with only a micron of glass between it and open air."

"I don't think anyone but you minds that."

"Oh, you did not just--"

"Head to the left up at the next junction."

"Hmm." She had to admit, his being completely inappropriate was taking her anxiety off of the task ahead. "Right. Doing this thing. Did you know this was an L1 job?"

"I have to admit, I don't know what that means."

"Company jobs each have designations. I've never paid much attention to them because I've never been given anything above an N7, and I've only ever had one of those. There are fifty-eight designations with differing levels of priority and access. L1 is the second highest. Just how much are you paying them?"

"My life is literally in their, and your, hands, Inez. I'm not going to cheap out on it."

"Where to now?" She'd reached another junction, and was starting to see more people. She was speaking lower because of it. Even so, her words caused the station to flash a directory straight in front of her. It took every muscle not to jump straight out of the suit. Well, she wasn't going to convince anyone that she wasn't a newcomer now.

She consulted with the map for a moment, and then tapped the air to close it. It was immediately replaced with an extremely explicit ad for "The hottest brothel in the Beehive." She pushed the proffered breasts away and the window closed.

"Why does every ad board think I need sex?" she muttered.

"I'll leave that one alone," Bolivar said over the ear-piece.

"Asshole," she said, as sotto voce as possible. "Alright, I can get there from here. You said he's young, with steel gray hair and actor good looks. I've seen ten of them so far."

"Sadly, folks in that line of work rarely provide headshots."

Inez assessed her surroundings. Whether the station's architecture intentionally referred to the Beehive or not, the interior design had no ambiguity. The most common color was honey yellow, with black stripes for accents. The first brothel she walked past (there were 18 on the station, and none were hurting for business as far as she could tell) was The Queen's Chambers. It frankly made her miss the shit brown of the Company docking wing.

She was heading for a small office complex called The Comb, where Foster Rios was going to be waiting for her. Based on the directory, she was going to be walking for a bit. She saw plenty of other people, women and men, in suits much like hers. Some carrying attache cases, some with bags, some with infrasonic blasters strapped to their waists.

Inez didn't have a weapon. She had only used a blaster a few times, and only once outside a controlled environment. It was a successful use, but she wasn't looking to relive the experience more than she had been already.

Still, it was unnerving to be around so many weapons displayed so openly. Sure, the marines had their weapons, but they also had uniforms and enough training not to go shooting people accidentally. Score one for military training, she thought, rolling her eyes at the absurdity. The Free Earth might kill her, but at least it wouldn't be by mistake.

Finally, she found her way to The Comb, and looked up the meeting ID that Rios had provided in the reception screen. It showed a series of red dots around corridors going deep into the complex. The floor also lit up with the red dots, so she closed the screen and proceeded down into the hexagonal maze.

She was used to angles being a bit odd (her own ship being triangular), but it was still disorienting. She had a vague idea of the number of turns she should be taking, but she found she lost count quickly. Finally, the red dots stopped in front of a plain, knobless door. She hadn't passed another soul since entering The Comb, which was also strange. The Beehive was a busy hub of commerce. Private, rentable conference rooms and offices seemed like something that would be in constant use. She tapped the single-icon input panel next to the door, and after a second, it opened.

The first thing she saw was that the room only had the one door. It also was generous to call it a room, being only slightly larger than the john on her rig. This meant that the handsome, yet short, human in the room was right up close and personal. He was an inch or two taller than Inez, with wavy silver hair (not natural), and piercing green eyes (also not natural).

Without saying anything, he handed her a business card. "Foster Rios, Ident 09-23##8-Σ." The card pulsed with an encrypted verification procedure. She handed it back to him, knowing it now said, "Gidget Perez, Ident 88-02*#8-Γ". (Bolivar had painted that Ident onto her right hand figuring Rios would use that type of ID verification.)

He looked at the card and nodded. He then indicated one of the two seats, separated by a slim table, and Inez sat down.

"You can't be too careful these days," the man said, taking his own seat. "All kinds of people out there."

"Oh, absolutely, Mr. Rios."

"Please, call me Foster."

"You can call me Gigi."

A smile traced the edges of his lips. "So you're looking for a fabricator?"

"Yes. It needs to be small enough to be portable, but powerful enough to produce materials quickly."

"How small are we talking?"

"It needs to fit in the same space as a TC-801, but twice as much output." This was what Bolivar had told her, and she did her best to sound like she had at least half a clue on the subject.

"That's not going to be cheap."

"Used is preferable."

"Perhaps, but more traceable." Inez didn't take her eyes off the man, but she couldn't get any sort of a read on him. His face remained blank while he browsed through options. "Since you've contacted me on the recommendation of Ingmar, I'm going to guess you want something that can't be easily traced. This narrows down the options quite a bit."

"I don't want to cheap out, but I don't want to overpay." She was bargaining with someone else's money, and no matter what he said, price was going to be an object at some point.

"I think I have what I need. You can go check into your hotel and I will contact you once I have an update."

"Great. Would you also be able to get ahold of a pair of Vascom XL personal comlinks? We have some other small asks as well."

"Should be simple enough."

"Excellent. Then I will await your comms." Inez rose and held out her hand. Rios stood and shook it perfunctorily. The door behind Inez opened, and she was back in the corridor. There were green dots now helpfully pointing the way back to the entrance.

Inez had peeled off the business suit and was back in her usual underclothes. She had availed herself of the shower and was now hopping through vid feeds looking for something to pass the time. The earpiece was also off, resting on the bedside table. This was a very nice hotel room, but it reminded her of the ridiculous opulence of the Admiral's estate. His first wife had designed it, but never got to live in it. She was killed in a space transport accident right around the time that the Admiral had been introduced to the daughter of one of his colleagues, later his second wife and Sara's mother.

Not that it was a shock the man was a murderous bastard. Sometimes, though, just how blatant it had been was breathtaking.

Inez was laying on the bed, just about to give up looking for something to watch, when the picture changed. It was Sara, back at her console.

"Hey, bee."

"Hey yourself. That was a bit terrifying earlier."

"It honestly doesn't happen that often." Inez sighed. "Don't give me that look, bee. I'm fine."

"And I'm Brother Lin's daughter. I need you to take care of yourself. Don't run yourself ragged for my sake. If anything happens to you, I won't be able to forgive myself."

"Same." Inez sighed again. "I need to know you're all right, or I won't be able to think straight."

"Speaking of thinking straight, your man Bolivar forwarded me a picture of you in a business suit."

"Oh gods."

"Damn, girl."

Inez rolled her eyes. Sara stuck out her tongue.

"What were your impressions of the facilitator?"

"He was kind of, I don't know, blank? Like he didn't have a full personality." She remembered how he hadn't said anything until after the verification was done. "I mean, he didn't seem dangerous, just a little off."

"That makes sense. I'm assuming you've never had to work with one before." It was a statement, but it hung in the air.

"It's never really come up in my deliveries."

"Facilitators usually fall into one of two camps. They're either overly gregarious and eager to please to a fault, or they're blank slates. The latter is usually because they had some really low-cost implants and it impacts their emotional output."

Inez shuddered. "I never want an implant in my brain. Ever."

"If you spend the money for quality, it's actually pretty seamless."

"As I said."

"They can't control your thoughts with a cranial implant."

"Maybe not control, but they sure as hell can change your mind."

Inez had to admit that Sara looked better than she had a few days ago. She had color in her cheeks now. She was smiling more easily. Then again, so was Inez. If she looked at it sideways and with one eye closed, she could almost see the two of them being together again. Almost, but not quite.

"So you're waiting on Rios. Any idea when he's going to get back to you?"

"He just said to leave it to him, so, any time between now and ten years from now."

"The decades do start to collect, don't they?"

"Will I be able to see you after this? I mean, assuming I don't get captured and dropped into a pit."

Sara smiled, and it was like no time at all had passed. "I think we can arrange that."

The bed was somehow too hard and too soft at the same time. She was used to her bed on the rig, so this hotel was wrong in just about every way. Leave it to her to find luxury uncomfortable.

After trying to sleep for an hour, she gave up. She grabbed a beer out of the cabinet and cracked it open. The walls were soundproof, which just led to the feeling of things being off. She could always hear her rig. It was a deep thrum that was never not there. Out in the hustle and bustle of the station, it was easier to ignore, but this silent room was too much.

She turned the display back on, looking for something that would work for background noise. She finally settled on a documentary about something called a penguin. The narrator had a soothing baritone voice, and Inez settled back onto the bed. The ice world where these penguin creatures lived looked like a place she would not want to settle down. The babies were cute, though. Little gray fluffballs that were far more awkward than you might expect.

The adults looked regal, even though they had flippers instead of arms and stubby legs. Inez found herself getting sucked into the story in the documentary. She was also finally getting sleepy.

Naturally, that's when the comm link chimed. She fumbled with it and finally got it in her ear.

"Yes?"

"Ms. Perez, meet me in an hour at the Honey Pot. I've got an update." It was Rios. She would just need to figure out what the hell the Honey Pot was.

Now fighting off sleepiness, Inez made her way to the hub of the station in order to cross over to the correct section for her meeting with Rios. She wasn't going back to her room, so she had the hotel send her things to the rig.

The Honey Pot advertised the best erotic entertainment in the station. Before she got there, she stopped at the Green Bean (not in the theme, but they were a chain) for as large a cup of coffee as they could make. She took it slightly sweet and black ("Like us," she would say to Ihuoma when they would go out for coffee), and the cup was 750 ml, so if this didn't jump start her brain, nothing would.

There were other stimulants, but coffee was always her first go-to. From the first time that Sara had brought her a cup, she was hooked. She just couldn't afford the equipment to roast it on the rig, and if she got it already roasted, gods knew how old it would be.

Though, if this was successful, she'd have a lot of euan to spend on some things for herself. Not to mention a fabricator to build some interesting equipment.

Right, focusing on the job. She had already finished half of her coffee by the time she reached the Honey Pot. It didn't look like much from the outside, just a pair of yellow doors with a view screen bouncer (a very limited AI). She waved her bank chip in front of it, and the doors opened.

Immediately, she was assaulted by the noise. The music was discordant, with an angry beat and incomprehensible lyrics. It was dark, but there were lasers cutting through the smoky air. Inez took a deep breath and stepped in.

In a room full of naked and nearly naked beautiful people dancing and fucking and whatever else they wanted, Rios stood out for being completely uninteresting. It only took a moment for her to locate the facilitator, face angled down at a pad that was clearing giving him some up to the moment information. Most of the other customers were at least watching the action going on around them, if not actively participating.

She set her coffee down on his table, and he looked up.

"Ah, Ms. Perez." Inez was a little surprised that she could hear him over the music. He must have some sort of fine band amplifier for his voice as one of the implants.

"What do you have for me?" She was fairly certain that was what she asked, though she definitely couldn't hear herself. She slid into the seat across from him. Frankly, the location made sense, with the noise and activity making it hard to listen in.

"It's a TKE 7500. It's about three cm wider than the TC-801, but runs 98% faster than the TC, and at significantly higher efficiency. It's 5 years old, but the scans indicate it's in top function."

"That should work here. Is it on the station?"

"Yes, they can deliver it to your berth."

"No need. I'll have my mechanotron pick it up. What's the damage?"

"85 euan."

Inez's eyes must have gone wide at that point, because Rios gave his first reaction of any sort that she had seen.

"I talked them down from 107."

Inez's earpiece chirped, and she heard Bolivar's voice. "Take him up on the offer."

"Right," she said, replying to both of them. "That will work for our needs."

"I'll just need your imprint here," he said, holding out the pad. She took out the bank chip and pressed it to the pad, and it showed 95 euan being transferred out. The extra ten was the man's fee. At least it wasn't her own money.

"Excellent. I'll have them await your automaton. They are at berth 50809."

"It was a pleasure doing business with you."

"And you."

Inez turned to rise from the table, and was immediately greeted by an erect cock at eye level. "Not now, thank you," she said, maneuvering around the two people who had encroached. She might have gone for it at another time, but this was a strange time for her, to say the least. She made her way back to the exit and to the much more sterile corridor. Her ears were still ringing from the noise in the club. She did not envy the automatons who had to clean that place.

Right now, what she wanted most was to get off the damn station. She wanted to get back into her own clothes, maybe have Lui braid her hair after giving it a thorough disinfecting. In fact, her whole body could probably use that. The disinfecting, not the braiding.

She was back in the middle of the station, amongst the dozens of people conducting their business. The station was an all hours business, and nearly every part of it was busy. People were going every which way, which actually made it easier to see the two people who were casually maintaining distance with her.

"I think I have a tail."

"I've been saying."

"I have someone following me. Jerk."

"Can you lose them?"

"I've never tried losing someone who's following me, so I'm just trying to act natural. Is Lui getting the equipment?"

"I just sent it out."

"How would anyone have figured out that I'm doing anything? I mean, I have a healthy sense of paranoia, but..."

"I haven't used that bank chip in a long time," he said, thoughtfully. "I think this is my fault."

"Great. Is Lui in danger?"

"Not until they get to Rios. Rios will probably give you up without a second thought."

"That's comforting," she said, trying not to give away her concern. "I'm going to get more coffee, since I left mine in the sex club. There's a sentence I never expected to say."

She walked as calmly and nonchalantly as she could over to a different Green Bean from the one before, this time getting a giant iced coffee. As she left the kiosk, she casually looked back to where the two people following her, a man and a woman in generic outfits, being conspicuously inconspicuous. She turned away, back toward the direction she was walking (which was nowhere near her rig; she was taking the long way around), and she honestly didn't think she could describe them. She knew they were still on her tail, though.

"Inez," Bolivar cut into her thoughts. "Lui just reported back that it has the fabricator and is returning to the ship. Where are you going?"

"They're about twenty meters behind me. Consistently. The corridors here are all a bit too long to lose them by turning corners. Is there a restroom near here?"

"About fifty meters ahead on the right."

"Alright, is there anything showing a vent or access tunnel?"

About thirty seconds passed without an answer. "No, nothing like that. There is a storage cube. It'll be tight."

"How tight?"

"I don't know how to answer that, based on the diagram."

"Well, I'm here now."

"Once you've entered, you will see it along the back wall."

She looked at the back wall, and realized that it was literally about 15 cm wide. "You have a more optimistic view of my ability to fit places than I do. Fuck."

There was a noise from one of the stalls. The door opened, and an automaton trundled out. There was a cart against the wall that must be its supplies.

"Another plan."

She opened the door on the side of the cart, and there was just enough space for her to sit, if she wasn't too concerned about breathing. She managed to jam herself in and grab her coffee. The Automaton shut her in (barely missing her fingers) and pushed the cart toward the door (she imagined, she couldn't see anything). Her neck was not going to forgive her for this.

She heard the door open and two sets of footsteps come in. The bot continued pushing to the exit, and behind her she heard the stall doors being slammed open. The automatons were ubiquitous on the station. Nobody paid them any mind. By the time they realized that they lost her, she would be half a kilometer away..

6

A hot blanket was draped over Inez. She was face down, letting the pain killers and the heat fix what the janitor's cart had done to her. When she'd crawled out of it, every part of her hurt. She was barely able to stand, let alone acknowledge Sven when he said a package had been delivered for her. That was the communicators, the raw materials, the skyn, and some more beer.

No doubt he figured she had run herself ragged at the sex clubs and was now doing the walk of shame back to her L1 assignment.

Lui had arrived not long after with the fabricator, and was currently working on installing it. Once again, she was sad not to have a shower on this ship. Maybe instead of a coffee roaster, she would spend the bonus on a sonic massage cleaner.

Bolivar had gotten the rig underway and plugged the blanket into the ship's power.

"I was so recently so very healthy," Inez mumbled into the pillow.

Lui patted her head gently with one of its manipulator arms.

"Thanks," she managed, and drifted off to sleep.

When she woke up, she felt warm and tingly. But not drunk warm and tingly. Must be the blanket and the drugs. She also felt like she could actually move, which was far better than what she had been dealing with.

"What time is it?"

"You've been asleep for about five hours."

"Is that all? Wake me up in a week."

"Sadly, we don't have a week. We're nearing the neighborhood of Earth."

Inez made a face. "Are you sure you want to go there? I've heard it's a shit hole."

"It is a shit hole. But yes, I must."

"Fine." She pushed herself up into a sitting position. The bottle of pain pills was next to her, so she fished two out and swallowed them dry.

"I've been following your Sara's directions on modifying the communicators. They are an interesting idea, and if they work, you might have given the forces of good a new tool."

She shrugged and nodded, still not quite at full thinking capacity. "'Forces of good' may be too optimistic. But 'forces working against evil' doesn't quite have the same ring, does it?"

There was a food bar and a glass of water next to her bed, so she opened the bar and took a small bite. She was hungry, but the sort of hungry that might turn to nausea if she did anything too quickly. It didn't taste like anything, which was actually a bit reassuring.

"Where are we on the plan?"

"We are twelve hours outside of the home system defenses. The new transponder coding is in place. We should be clear until we reach the docking station."

They would be decelerating by now. Free Earth didn't allow FTL inside the orbit of the Kuiper belt, so they would need to make those adjustments. The Free Earth armada had orders to shoot down anything going faster than light (other than their own ships, of course), mostly to avoid a ship crashing into Earth at light speed. The devastation that would cause was immense.

Of course, they didn't have that restriction in any other star system, so the occasional FTL-winter had occurred on colony planets.

"Fabulous. So, just under a day. Is Lui working on the uniforms and augments?"

"The fabricator has finished one of the uniforms and is creating the second. From there, the augments should only take about two hours to mock up."

"So now we just have to figure out getting down to the surface sometime before the next decade. Jumping the line would be fairly simple if we were actually maintenance. Our idents need to be perfect if we're going to get through."

Inez drank the glass of water down in one motion. It didn't quite wash away the chalkiness of the food bar.

"We also," she continued, worrying her bottom lip with her teeth, "need to act like maintenance. I assume they're just as odd on Earth as they are anywhere else." The maintenance workers that Inez had encountered were all business, but deeply disinterested in anything happening around them. It was not unlike how Rios had been, come to think of it. It probably had to do with their augments keeping them apart from the world. They had their own thing going on, so the outside was less real to them.

"Have you ever acted?"

Half an hour later, Inez was convinced that German Bolivar was congenitally incapable of not smiling.

"You are bored. Your general feeling is ennui. This life is secondary to you. Your emotions are inconvenient, and you eschew inconvenience. It's the only way you can survive being a maintenance worker."

She watched him try to reconfigure his face into something more neutral, and it was painful.

"You exist in the feed and only in the feed. Your work is only a means to an end, and the euan you earn go into more upgrades for your connection. You view the automatons you maintain as little more than a nuisance."

With the mustache gone, his upper lip looked naked. It was like this was something she wasn't supposed to see. And still, he was smiling.

"What the hell are you smiling about?"

"It's just my face. It doesn't matter what I'm feeling, my face smiles."

"And your eyes twinkle?"

"No, that is amusement."

"Asshole." She sighed and rolled her eyes. "What do we need to do to get you in character?"

"Get me to Earth. That is all that I will need to lose my smile."

Somehow that statement conveyed everything that needed to be said. As he was saying it, she watched his eyes darken and the corners of his mouth droop.

"You aren't looking forward to this." It was a statement. Something she'd guessed at but hadn't really seen like she was seeing it now.

"This is going to be one of the hardest things I do in my life. And I don't know if the risk is worth the outcome."

Inez indicated the chair with a nod of her head, and the older man sat down. "Ten years ago, I was a slave. An orphan. A stupid teenager in love. Ten years ago, my owner decided to attack me, by himself, while completely shit-faced drunk. He was a mean drunk and he'd been drummed out of the navy a year before.

"This time, when he attacked, I fought back. In the struggle, I got his blaster and shot his head off."

Bolivar nodded. He'd clearly been around enough infrasonic blasters to know what they were capable of.

"Did your home use slaves?"

"Technically, no. But that left a lot of wiggle room. There were indentured servants living out their contracts. There were prisoners doing work for pennies. There were all kinds of shit work for shit pay and I wasn't as cognizant of it as I could have been."

"Yeah, I see that a lot. Citizens are never as aware of how their coffee gets grown, only if it's too hot to drink."

"So how did you manage to get away?"

"Sara, of course. She hacked, as you said, to change the Admiral's will, and she's good enough at it that they couldn't tell. That gave her mother a pittance, around ten thousand euan, and told her to leave the compound, and everything else went to Sara. Including me, and all the other slaves."

"So you were freed. What of the others?"

"She sold the compound and released them, giving them all a hundred and fifty euan to try and make a life. Not much, but enough to get away and get their freedom notarized."

When Sara had offered Inez more, she turned her down. She regretted that sometimes. It was a couple months after she'd left, and she was already on the ag planet growing rye. She didn't know how Sara had tracked her down, but at that point Inez had wanted to leave that whole chapter of her life behind and be a new woman. She was sixteen, and a whole new universe was in front of her.

It turned out to just be the same universe, though, full of the same shit coming from new people. The names had changed, technically the status had changed, but other than getting a few euan here and there, she was just as chained.

"You know, it would have been a simple thing for her to let you go, but keep everything else. I think your Sara has a good heart."

"Yeah," she said, rubbing at a twinge in her neck. "I suppose it would have."

The computer chimed in at that point. "Prešli smo marsovski obod. Upočasni na petindvajsetsto kilometrov na sekundo."

"I think we've just passed Mars. Time to work."

● - - - ▬▬▬▬▬ - - ▬ ılı((◉))ılı ▬ - - ▬▬▬▬▬ - - - ●

Ten hours later, Inez and Bolivar were sitting on a bench, looking straight forward, with Lui on the ground between them. The station orbiting over Oslo was a giant, brutal block, with four hundred decks of functionaries, secretaries, flunkies, toadies, and middle-management. These were the Free Earth people not important enough to work on the planet, but too important to work out in the galaxy.

Earth had fifteen billion people living on it, and another thirty billion between Earth and Mars on stations, patrol ships, and mining convoys. Mars itself had seven billion.

All of that meant that they were crowded here. Severely crowded. This station alone had 17 million people (Citizens, non-citizens, slaves) living and working on it. There were literally six times as many people on this station than had settled Hibiscus Prime. Three full decks were dedicated to the growing of food for everybody, and those were, of course, farmed by slaves.

(Inez tried not to think about it when they had received their food rations. All workers on the station were entitled to food, based on their jobs. As maintenance people, she and Bolivar were given thirty meal bars for the week. Higher level workers were more likely to get better, and more recognizable, food.)

Lui had received a makeover, with Free Earth Maintenance logo decals affixed to its sides. Bolivar, who truly looked like a different man without his bushy mustache, also had a transparent screen in front of his left eye, which was showing him random data. Screens like this were common for maintenance, to show important information about how to fix things, or what was wrong. It was attached to his temple with the skyn to make it look like an actual augmentation.

Inez had a full face visor attached behind the ears. This was actually functional, and she was getting information from Lui. The skyn made it look like it was tied into her head on each side. She also had a glove augmentation that looked really technical, but in actuality did nothing except remind her to twitch her fingers occasionally.

They had arrived at the station about four hours prior, and had put in a priority taxi request at that time. The taxi kiosk had told them they would need to wait twenty-four hours before they would be given a berthing number, where they would then go to find out how long of a wait they would have before getting a seating assignment. The whole thing could take a week, if not a month, depending on the administrators involved.

The kiosk hadn't noticed Lui transmitting the code that Sara had given them to help speed things along, so they had already managed to get their berth assignment, and were now waiting for their seating assignment. Inez and Bolivar had barely spoken two words to each other in this time, and would need to stay that way until they were in Oslo.

Lui was also generating the signals masking the fact that Inez and Bolivar didn't have processors wired into their brains. Most people in Maintenance needed to have a processing cache to deal with sudden info dumps about the units they were maintaining. It was yet one more reason that Inez didn't want to be in Maintenance.

They were cut off from Sara, and would be the entire time they were on Earth. There was no one to swoop in and rescue them if this didn't work. Bolivar and Inez each had their comm bracelets on, but they wouldn't be any actual use for communication, after being altered to block the sensor traces they would leave behind on the planet.

Lui flashed a message in Inez's visor. "We're up," she said, and stood. She walked forward without looking to Bolivar, just strode straight to the desk. The desk clerk, also with visible augmentations, sent a message at Inez, which Lui picked up and sent to her. Inez raised her arm, as did Bolivar, and the clerk scanned both.

A new message flashed in Inez's view, giving their itinerary. They would be leaving for Earth in three hours.

She flashed three fingers at Bolivar, who was now present in her periphery. She then made her way down to the concourse where the taxi would be picking them up. The taxis were fifty seat elevators, gliding up and down nanofilament cables, and were completely insufficient to the number of people traveling to the planet. A taxi would take half a day to descend or ascend, and would need to be repositioned in place and filled with people within an hour before the next one arrived. It was mostly done by automatons.

There hadn't been an emergency in a taxi in over a hundred years. The taxis in service now were the same ones that had been running then. Inez tried not to think about the last time she was in a nearly hundred-year-old ship. It hadn't ended well.

Thankfully, she'd gotten off before it blew up. Still, she didn't know their maintenance schedules, and really didn't want to look into it.

Despite being bored (and the heist vids that Sara had sent her along with everything else had never included the long stretches of boredom while The Plan was happening), the time passed fairly quickly, and they managed to duck into the taxi around the two marines who were yelling at the clerk about getting bumped to a later (based on the conversation, about a month later) taxi.

This was it. There was no going back at this point. Earth lay below, which they had a great view of through the clear bulkhead in front of them. The main colors visible were brown and chrome. It was exactly the sort of shithole that Inez expected.

The tallest buildings, several kilometers high, were carbon scrubbers that were completely inadequate to the task of cleaning the air. The city would have more effective scrubbers, so they wouldn't have to worry about breathing, but it was hardly encouraging.

The twelve hour journey seemed like it would be a gentle controlled fall. This meant Inez was unprepared when the taxi started, the artificial gravity cut off, and her stomach lurched into her throat.

No one else around her reacted, so this must be normal. Inez did her best to control her breathing, and she felt Bolivar reach out and squeeze her hand where it couldn't be seen. She noted where the restrooms were, just in case.

7

Inez tried not to gawp at the city around her. There were some cities that had sprung up on colony planets, but nothing as crowded, massive, or overbearing as Oslo. Even here, less than a mile from the central palace, where security wasn't just tight but omnipresent, the throng of people was more even than was on the station.

Their uniforms and the presence of a mechanotron allowed a certain deference, and people made way for them, though just barely.

"Blackout," she said, assuming that Bolivar would hear her. He clearly did, as she saw him raise his arm to turn on the communicator. If anyone was watching them through a camera, they would have disappeared. Two people in a crowd of thousands winking out of existence, the hole left by their invisibility barely large enough to register on any trace.

To counter the trace any further, the two of them then split up. Inez went right, and Bolivar and Lui went left. The plaza where they were walking, right outside of the taxi station, was between two wide avenues filled with personal vehicles. To the north, which was the general direction that both of them were headed, there was a gleaming spire of chrome kilometers tall and filled with corporate accountants for the Free Earth State Bank. The top was invisible, shrouded in the brown clouds that made up most of the sky.

From a distance, it was all chrome, but up closer, Inez could see that the sides of the building were windows with a reflective coating. She could see men, women, and others, in their skin-tight business suits and ridiculous hairstyles.

There was a street-level coiffurie in the building, and dozens of people were getting their hair extended, colored, and raised. She'd seen a few of these hairstyles on the station, but they seemed the norm for anyone who didn't need to worry about getting it caught in anything at the job. Coiffuries were also ridiculously expensive, but she had a feeling that if you didn't pay to have stupid hair, you would never get a promotion.

Past the FESB was another broad avenue. As Inez got to the corner, she saw that Bolivar and Lui hadn't gotten here yet. She waited in a crowd of pedestrians, all looking for a signal that they could cross the street. On the next city block was a grand lawn. There were no green spaces in Oslo, as far as Inez could tell, except for this lawn leading up to the palace. There were elm trees all around and a reflecting pool in the middle, but it just looked muddy brown.

The signal came and Inez crossed the six lanes of traffic with the hundreds of others, and then forced her way left to walk up where she had a feeling that Bolivar and Lui had gone. With the communicators running, it would be impossible to shout out to Lui over the rig's comms, so she was taking it on faith that they would be there.

Something had started to bug her about the people around her, and not just their hair or lack of interest. She couldn't put her finger on it, though. It reminded her of Rios, but not exactly. She chalked it up to the war, figuring that she would have expected people on Earth to be more worried about the Hands of the Gods than people on Podunk worlds out on the outer belt were.

She finally spotted Bolivar and, after a few seconds, Lui. She put aside that wondering as she increased her pace to get to them more quickly. She was surprised at how relieved she was to see them. She hadn't realized she'd been worrying.

They weren't walking straight into the palace, even though it was right there. Bolivar's meeting was close (excruciatingly close) to the palace, but they were going to a subbasement in the Colonial Ministry building, which was in a carve-out in a corner made by the palace and the lawn.

Traveling with Lui was the only way to make sensors pick up on them. They walked straight past the security desk (their uniforms did most of the work for them there) and to a bank of elevators. Lui summoned one for them, and they entered.

Once inside, the elevator already knew where they were going and had the clearances for it. Another gift from Sara so that Lui wouldn't need to physically break into the elevator's systems. With the doors closed, and cameras not able to see or hear them, Inez relaxed.

"So, once you've been successfully delivered, your people will come get your cargo hold from me, right?"

"I promise, your hands will be quite clean of me."

"What is it that you're planning, anyway? Why come all the way here to the center of hell to do this clandestine shit? Encrypted messages exist."

"I'm surprised you didn't ask sooner." Bolivar's eyes had opened wider, to punctuate something.

"I didn't trust there to be a lack of listening devices. I'm paranoid like that."

"But here?"

"Here, if they're following us or listening, we're fucked anyway."

Bolivar tilted his head in acknowledgment of the point. "This isn't just a discussion. Things are going to happen, and soon. No," he held his hands out, "I cannot go into details. Suffice it to say that things are in motion."

"I'm not a revolutionary," Inez said, looking down at her hands. "I'm not. I'm just trying to survive."

"You don't need to be. You will be well away from here before anything happens."

Inez felt relief at his words, and then almost physically recoiled. "Gods, why do I trust you? I don't even know you."

The elevator stopped. They were about 700 meters below the surface, and deep in the heart of the secret operations of Free Earth. They resumed walking in silence, letting Lui trail behind them as would probably usually be the case. They reached a door and Bolivar pulled out a chip and pressed it to the lock. It clicked open.

Inez reached inside her uniform for the job pad. She held it out to him, and he placed his thumb denoting that the delivery was made.

"Good luck, German," she said as she put the pad away.

"And you, pata." The door opened, and he stepped through.

● ▪ ▪ ▪ ━━━━━ ▪▪ ━ ıı((◉))ıı ━ ▪▪ ━━━━━ ▪▪▪ ●

"Why do I trust him?" Inez asked Lui as the elevator took them back up to the main level. "I don't trust anybody. Sara. I trust one person. Ihuoma, two people. But that's it. And you, of course. Are you people?"

A message popped up on her visor: "Which question should I answer?"

"Now you're fucking with me. Thanks."

They made their way out to the street and disappeared into the throng. She turned off the comms bracelet, and almost immediately heard the rig message her.

"Auto-undock sequence initiated for cargo pod."

"I assume the English won't last?"

"Aš nežinau, apie ką jūs kalbate."

"As I figured."

Now, she just needed to get back to the station without being noticed, and she was golden.

Inez bumped into someone who had stopped right in front of her. The woman had a blank expression on her face, more so than what she had seen on the other pedestrians. "Sorry," she muttered, but the woman didn't react. Inez turned to go around her, and there was another person there not moving.

"The fuck?"

She went the other way, and ran into another human statue. She turned around. Nobody was moving. Each one had the same blank face, like they had been turned off.

She knew it was too late, but she turned the comms device back on to try and give her even a little bit of time before everything caught up with her. "Lui, go to the station. Get to the ship. I'll meet you there."

Lui popped up a message in front of her, since she was blocking comms signals now. "I must protect."

"No, please, I can't get away if I'm worrying about you, too. Go." Lui stayed where it was. "Please."

After a moment's hesitation, it backed away and then started off through the crowd at a speed Inez was a little jealous of at the moment.

Now, it was time to get moving.

She stayed low. They couldn't follow her implants or any electronics on her, couldn't even measure heart rate and brain activity, but they could see her if they looked. The people being frozen in place was actually a bit of a blessing here, since they weren't reacting when she bumped into them. They may as well have been trees in a thick forest.

She heard a drone coming in from the direction of the palace. She froze in place. The drone wouldn't have analog visual sensors, probably. Still, she didn't want to chance it.

The drone moved off to another section of the plaza, and Inez pushed through more people. Other than the buzz of the drone, the plaza was silent, which is why she was able to hear the many footsteps of guards also coming in from the plaza.

Inez shrugged out of her uniform, revealing the business suit underneath. She also ripped off the visor and glove, wrapped them in the uniform, and carefully put them inside the carry-on bag that a man next to her had been pushing toward the space elevator terminal.

In a crouch, she made her way about ten meters to her right, away from where she'd heard the boots. She slowly stood, surrounded by people much taller than she was, and slipped the comms bracelet off her wrist. She deactivated it and let it drop to her foot, and then the ground, making very little noise.

She stood there, still as a statue among statues.

●∙∙∙ ▬▬▬▬ ∙∙ ▬ ιι((◉))ιι ▬ ∙∙ ▬▬▬▬ ∙∙∙●

An hour later, but just as suddenly as it had started, the people began moving again. It was clear that time had passed for them, as they stretched their arms and legs, which had been stuck in place. It was just as clear that this was something that happened from time to time, and while it was annoying to them, they were used to it.

Inez mimicked those around her, rolling her neck, making no eye contact, but still trying to look at people. It had to be something with their implants that allowed security to freeze them. That was the sort of thing that was going to give her nightmares for a long time.

She knew that she couldn't go to the terminal. They would expect her to try to leave that way. She had a bank chip with 80 euan on it, more than enough to get passage to another city with an elevator, and then she could contact the ship and have it autopilot to meet her there.

Right now, the thing she needed most was a map. There had to be a central over-land hub, and it was probably not far. Security would probably be looking for her there, but she reckoned that they didn't know exactly what she looked like. And if they did, then she'd deal with that when it came up.

This was a business district, so she looked for anything that appeared to be a banking terminal. She would be able to use it to also look up local information, things like hotels and dining and, oh, where's the hub to get the fuck out of here?

The bank chip was Bolivar's. He'd insisted she hold onto it to make sure she got back to the station. Hopefully, this didn't have the same issue the one she'd used on Beehive did, or this was going to be a very short escape.

She finally saw a sign for a bank terminal, next to the bank building (go figure), about fifty meters away. She strode that way with a purpose, again copying those around her who, now that the excitement was over, were setting about their days again.

Evenings, actually. Inez realized that she didn't have a grasp of the local time, but it was getting darker in the sky, so that either meant night was coming or a storm was, and as bad as the sky looked, she knew that the weather control wouldn't let it rain in the middle of Oslo.

There was a man using the terminal when she got there, so she lined up off to the side to wait for him to finish. She was waiting for over five minutes before he finally finished up. The man turned around and Inez realized he was wearing the uniform of palace security. Fuck.

Maybe he wouldn't recognize her? No, that luck wasn't going her way, as he turned his gaze straight at her. She spun around and there were ten other security officers, each reaching for their stunners. They also had infrasonic pistols, but thankfully they weren't reaching for them. Yet.

Inez spun back around and charged at the man from the terminal. She caught him in the center of the chest with her shoulder, which clearly winded him. Then she spun around again and ran into the throng, away from all of the guards she had seen.

She didn't know where she was going. Right now, she was just going away. She got a message from her rig, but she couldn't hear it over her heart beating and she probably wouldn't have understood it, either. Still, a thought.

"Ship, using audio pings differentiated by volume, let me know if I'm going toward or away from the nearest overland hub."

"បានប្រតានទក្រុម។"

She heard a faint ping, getting fainter. "Alright," she murmured, and veered off to the left. The volume increased, so she pushed off further in that direction. Eventually, she reached one of the broad avenues, and she ran right out into it. The many speeding vehicles all automatically adjusted course to avoid her, and she got to the other side.

On this side, there were many fewer people, so hiding would be that much harder. She kept to her run as she was going around the next building, with the pinging getting that much louder.

If they saw her (there was no proof that they did; there was no way that they didn't), they would probably figure out where she was going. But that was a risk she had to take right now. The sky was almost completely dark, and the street lights were casting a sickly sort of light onto the path she was taking.

What the light showed her was that she was nearly out of other people to hide amid. With the ridiculous hair and tight business suits, Inez was keenly aware that she didn't fit, especially running and making a scene. If there was anything she noticed while being on Earth for the last few hours, it was that nobody made a scene, ever.

Everyone was equally outlandish and so no one stood out, except for the girl trying desperately to be invisible. Invisibility was her only shield, and she knew that was gone. Lui was probably already on the elevator going up, and Bolivar was at his clandestine meeting. She was the last loose end, and if she could get to the over-land hub, she would be able to slip away.

At the insistence of the pinging in her ear, she turned a corner, and she could see the hub. It was brightly lit and inviting, and she wanted nothing more than to sprint for the doors. But she was spent. It was about a hundred meters away, and so she changed to as fast a walk as she could manage. At fifty meters, she could see a scrum of people around the main entrance. At thirty, she could see their uniforms. Fuck.

She turned and quickly walked out of their field of vision. There had to be a side entrance, or a space where she could hide until they gave up looking for her. Frankly, she wasn't even sure why they were after her, whether it was for Bolivar, the data core, killing the Admiral, or if they just didn't like her. In the end, that wasn't really important.

There was nobody on this street. That was good? Wasn't good? She saw that there was an open door about twenty meters down, though, and decided to make a run for it. If she could get in, if no one was there, she could wait it out.

She got to the door, and saw two people standing over a piece of equipment. She felt the air pressure around her drop, making her immediately giddy. Then the air cannon hit and she flew across the street into a glass wall.

8

The Admiral was bearing down on her, with his cricket bat in his left hand, down at his side. It was painted in the colors of the colony's team, teal and brown. He'd never played cricket, she knew, but he had swung that bat.

"Come back here, you bitch." His voice was a growl, predatory, drunk but in full control.

Inez was running through the hall. She was sixteen years old. Eleven years old. Five. Twenty-seven.

"I enjoyed fucking that girl, no matter how dark she was. And you're just like her."

That girl. Her mother. Who was a whole-ass woman by the time Inez was born, but that didn't matter. Any slave he owned was "girl" or "boy". And while any poor person could become a slave, the Admiral had a particular inclination in his purchases. The higher bred you were, the darker your slaves.

Inez hid under a table in the hall, but the Admiral yanked it off the floor and tossed it aside. He was monstrously large, and Inez was so much smaller. "Get her on the gurney," he snarled. "Stabilize her."

Inez caught snatches of people talking, but mostly it was as understandable as her ship's computer. She was lying down, but she wasn't still. She was being moved somewhere.

She definitely had a concussion. Two in the space of a few weeks was not the best thing for her. At least last time she'd immediately been taken to a medbay. She had no idea where she was now.

The lights were bright, and she needed to keep her eyes closed or the pain in her head would knock her out again. She felt very strongly that she needed to be awake.

She was very sure about some things, like that she was on Earth, and that she had finished her job, and that these people were not good people trying to help her. Her job was, fuck, what was it? Right, it was delivering someone. Who? Gods dammit, all she could see was a thick mustache.

She realized she was being restrained, held in place by the gurney, and she could feel the electrical stings of probes working on her head. Either it was a bad attempt at making her compliant, or she was getting medical attention. She really hoped it was the second one.

She could feel the stiff cloth of the gurney on her scalp. The fuckers shaved her fucking head. That's it, it was time to burn this place down. As soon as she could move.

Based on the equipment in use, she had to assume it was a medical facility, but it didn't smell like a hospital.

There was a staleness to the air. This had to be a medsuite in a prison or something.

All this thinking was exhausting, and Inez dozed off again.

• ▪ ▪ ▪ ▬▬▬▬ ▪ ▪ ▪ ━ ιι((◉))ιι ━ ▪ ▪ ▬▬▬▬ ▪ ▪ ▪ •

Running down the street, away from the Admiral and the palace guards. Forcing her legs to keep moving. But she was so small, and the road was so long. She was only a child, and she was in so much trouble. Her mom would protect her, if she could just get to her.

The thought of her mother gave her strength. She was a teenager and could outrun an old man and the palace dogs to get to the rye fields. She could lose them in the fields, Zzrft promised her. She could lose them forever.

She sped around the corner, and there was Sara, sixteen and healthy and ready to run with Inez as far as she had to. Inez grabbed her hand and pulled her along, and she could see the fields, see freedom. Then, suddenly, she couldn't breathe, and then she felt the impact.

• ▪ ▪ ▪ ▬▬▬▬ ▪ ▪ ▪ ━ ιι((◉))ιι ━ ▪ ▪ ▬▬▬▬ ▪ ▪ ▪ •

Air cannon! Those fuckers used an air cannon. Air cannons were illegal on most colony worlds for crowd control, considering the level of injury they could cause. Either they weren't illegal here, or they just used them anyway.

Inez had a clear memory of the two people who were standing over the air cannon. One was a stocky, middle-aged man with short hair, while the other was a younger woman in baggy coveralls and her long hair in a tail.

Neither one was wearing the colors of the palace guard, city police, or the military. Given how they had seemed to know where she was headed in enough time to set up the cannon, was it possible that they weren't a part of the Free Earth at all?

She tried opening her eyes, which was a struggle. They didn't want to open, were afraid of the light. She forced one to open a crack, and there was only low-level light. Someone had turned the lights down, clearly. A few minutes were spent getting used to having her eyes open.

Then she tried raising her arm, which she was able to do. No restraints, then. She turned her head to the side to look around. She didn't feel her brain sloshing around inside her skull, so she figured they must have finished treating the concussion.

There was nothing she could see to identify where she was. The walls were plain white, and there didn't seem to be a door in any of them.

A cell, then. She looked down at her body, and saw that she was wearing a gray shirt and pants, far too large for her. If popular entertainment in the colonies was anything to go by, this was not a typical prison uniform for Free Earth detainees.

She got up and walked around. The cell was barely large enough for her bed and a commode, and she walked around, testing wall panels, to see if she could find where the door was. She couldn't.

She figured there must be cameras around. She stuck a finger in her ear and was surprised to find that the rig's communicator was still there. No signal, though, so something had to be blocking it.

"I know you can hear me," she said, startled by how loud she sounded. "I don't know what you want, but I doubt I can give it to you. I deliver packages for the Browns, that's it."

A wall panel slipped into the floor, revealing German Bolivar. He had regrown his mustache (good to know he had his priorities straight, for fuck's sake) and was standing patiently, holding a duffel bag out to her.

"What the fuck, Bolivar?"

"I know you're angry," he said, that accent of his softening something in Inez's chest, something she wanted very hard right now. "Come with me and I'll explain. And then you'll be free to go."

"I don't fucking trust you," she said, taking the bag.

"I know. But, you do."

And she did. Again. She trusted him despite every indication that he had fucked her over.

"Who do you work for?" she asked, slowly emerging from the cell.

"All in good time. Do you need anything? Coffee, perhaps?"

She really did need coffee, but she wasn't going to let him play the gracious host. "Don't fucking do that." Her anger was winning over the insidious trust that was trying to take hold in her chest, but it was a close thing.

After a short walk, they came into a room that looked like a command center from the vids. There were a dozen people there, including, she noted, the Colonial Affairs Secretary from the Free Earth. She was almost as ubiquitous an image as Brother Lin out in the colonies, but the image out there was of a much younger woman with dark hair. The woman before her had short salt and pepper hair and frown lines.

"This is the girl?" she asked, looking from Inez to Bolivar.

"Indeed."

"I'm going to need some damn explanations soon," Inez barked to the room.

"Of course. Inez, welcome to the resistance."

Inez stared hard at the older woman. Her anger and her resentment at being called a girl were fighting at her disbelief that someone that high up in Lin's cabinet was going to be any part of a resistance movement.

"I don't believe you," she said, finally.

Bolivar began, as though she hadn't spoken, "We knew you were in trouble when the signal to stop in place came down. I don't know exactly how they figured out you were bringing me here, but I knew we couldn't leave you to be discovered. I had an idea of where you would be headed, so we set up the air cannon."

Inez realized one of the other people in the room was the woman who'd been standing next to the cannon.

"That fucking hurt."

"You wouldn't have come willingly."

"I told you, I'm not a revolutionary."

"No, you're not," the Secretary said, sternly. "You're a liability to the resistance. By rights, we should have killed you, but German said not to."

"This all seems awfully well funded for a resistance movement. Not that I've been part of any before, but aren't they a little more ragtag usually?"

"Oh, we're being funded by the Free Earth," Bolivar said.

Inez let out a guffaw. "Of course you are."

"Secretary Voss is officially here as a spy in our ranks. She gives them just enough good intel that they don't suspect she is a traitor."

"Oh my gods. You're all insane. And I'm insane too, to be standing here listening to you."

"Don't fret, dear."

"Don't 'dear' me, asshole." It hurt to call him out. Why was it so hard? "I'm done. I'm just fucking done. Take me back to my cell, or let me go. I don't care."

She turned around, and found the air cannon woman standing in the doorway, blocking her. She spun back around the other way. "The Browns. They made delivering you a top priority. They're in on this, too."

"No, they aren't." This was the Secretary. "They are very useful idiots, though."

"Please, Inez," Bolivar said, and she stopped. You've been hurt by the Free Earth. Everyone you love has. You have to see that you can't keep running away."

"Oh, I can. I very much can." She ran away from the Admiral. She ran away from Sara. She ran away from Ihuoma. She ran... toward the Free Earth marines who held someone her own actions had put in danger. "What the fuck are you working on here? Because I've seen no evidence of a resistance."

A "Free" Earth where you couldn't even trust that you wouldn't get zapped and frozen in place by the implants that you were forced to have. There was no resistance to that, other than leaving as expeditiously as possible.

"You know what I saw out there? While I was trying to be a statue? They don't want to be free. They are perfectly happy here on this shithole of a planet, and there's no point in trying to save them."

The Secretary laughed once, and went back to what she had been doing before. Bolivar reached out to touch Inez's shoulder, and she twisted away from him.

"We know. This is a place that has selected its manner of enslavement, a level it's just comfortable with. Billions of people with nothing to look forward to. We can't save them."

"Then what the fuck are you doing?"

"We're trying to save the trillions of people who still have hope." He had positioned himself between Inez and the door, she noticed. "We're working for the Hands."

"What hands?" she said, reflexively. Then all warmth drained from Inez's body. This was... she didn't know what the fuck it was, but it wasn't good, and it was not something she'd ever suspected. She was rooted in place now.

"H--" she started, swallowed, took a breath, "how? No one knows the Hands. Nobody's seen one, interacted with their technology, haven't even spoken to one. Fuck, we don't even know what to call them."

"Nor have we," he said, hands raised, placating. "We work through an intermediary on Palestine."

"Are you sure? I wouldn't be that sure. They're a fucking black box. How do you know you aren't being used?"

"My hasty departure from that colony was because the intermediary tipped me off to an incoming Free Earth fleet. Lin finally decided to deal with the colonists."

"That was over a week ago, Bolivar. Wouldn't it have been on the news?"

"I've seen many colonies fall that did not make the news."

"I believe that you believe this. I would need more than some guy's insistence. I just--"

The bomb inside the air cannon woman went off at that point.

Inez couldn't hear anything. She was calling out, but she didn't know if she was making any noise. She was covered in blood. Some of it was hers, some of it was Bolivar's (he was still breathing, if shallowly), and some was the air cannon woman's. Her blood was over everything. Inez was momentarily glad that she'd had her hair shaved off.

It was wrong to say she couldn't hear anything. She heard ringing. It would be deafening if she wasn't already pretty sure her ear drums had burst. She crawled over to Bolivar (she was on the ground, she belatedly noticed) and checked his pulse. It was still there, but weak. She got her shoulder under his and managed to get him upright. He weakly pointed out to the hall, and she went, glad she couldn't hear as she walked through the remains of the woman.

She saw that he was pointing her to the medsuite that she had been in earlier. There were people running in and out and trying to figure out what had happened. Inez got him into the diagnostic chair and started it running.

Bolivar nodded, and then mouthed the word "Go." Maybe he said it, she still wasn't sure.

It took the better part of an hour to find an exit. No one was paying attention to her, which helped her move faster, but not being able to ask anyone which way was out was not helping.

When she got to the exit, it was a vent shaft with a ladder. If she was lucky, it would let her out somewhere that wouldn't immediately lead to her getting caught. If she had to estimate, she was about 150 meters below the surface. This was going to take a while.

A beep in her ear startled her almost enough to make her fall. After three hours of no sound, it was the loudest thing ever. She was about fifty meters from the top now. The beep came again. The earpiece from the ship! It must have saved that ear drum. She tapped her other ear and got nothing, so that one would wait until she was able to get it repaired.

"Ship, cancel last command."

The ship responded (barely at mumble volume) and the beeping stopped. Her last command was to beep louder if she was getting close to the hub. She was going to come out at the hub, and the security forces and palace guards would almost certainly grab her.

On the other hand, she'd already climbed this far, she may as well deal with it.

She honestly wasn't sure if her decision making was being affected by another concussion.

The light coming in said it was about mid-day, and she assumed it was simply the next day. Maybe they would have given up. Maybe they would assume she was dead after the bomb. That bomb had to be Free Earth. There was no one else it could be.

She was pretty sure she'd gotten all of the shrapnel (bone shrapnel, ewww) that she'd been hit with off of her. Based on what she saw of Bolivar's injuries, she figured there had to be some non-organic shrapnel in the bomb itself, too. Metal fragments, glass, anything that would cause lots of damage to squishy people.

Were these people foolish enough to work with the Hands? Well, clearly yes, since that's what they thought they were doing. It didn't make any sense, though. The Hands were powerful enough that they could probably wipe out Earth and the rest of the solar system without much effort.

It would make more sense if it was the Free Earth making them think it was the Hands, feeding them just enough through this Intermediary.

No, no, not getting involved.

Finally, she emerged from the vent shaft opening, which was about ten meters above the ground, but with a walkway over to a building. The hub building. She might somehow get free from here.

Now that she was out in the open (though, not immediately visible from the ground), she opened the duffel. Her regular jumpsuit, a bank chip, her job pad with the proof she needed of the completed job for the Company.

She got out of the bloody clothes she was wearing and into the jumpsuit. Just that small act made her feel more at ease.

She found a door on the roof of the hub, and found that it was unlocked. Time to fucking go.

9

The overland transit, a mag-lev train that did a soothing rocking motion, had very comfortable seats, and Inez listened to music in her good ear. She had contacted the rig, and was very happy to hear that Lui had made it back safely.

She was currently headed to Moscow. That was the next nearest space elevator taxi. She had managed to report back to the Company, reserve a medsuite chair on the space end of the elevator, and check her account. Bolivar had put the rest of his promised payment into her account. She was so close to actually owning her rig.

But she was also pissed off at the charming revolutionary for hire/damn fool. She had her thumb drawing the funds over to her loan, but stopped.

"Come on, Stanton, what are you doing?" She closed the bank window. That would hold.

Based on what she could see out the window, everywhere was covered in brown snow. This place really was a shithole. Was it always like this? The inconstant temperatures, areas that were completely unlivable ninety percent of the time, and the smell, everywhere, like each part of the planet was drenched in stale urine.

She should be in Moscow by nightfall, and then she would catch the next space elevator taxi up. That shouldn't take too long. The limits were really on people coming down to the planet, not on those getting the hell off of it.

It seemed like there were fewer people who wanted to leave than wanted to come. She couldn't even begin to imagine why they would want to be here. The architecture was awful, the temperature swung far to wildly, and, oh, the government were controlling pricks.

Fifteen billion people crammed into what areas were still livable after centuries of wars, terrorism, and global climate catastrophes, and people still preferred it to the deep stillness of space. Inez knew one thing only right now, and that was that she didn't belong on this planet.

The movement of the train finally led her down into a blissfully dreamless sleep.

She picked up some borscht and fried dumplings from a street vendor. This might be the last real food she had for a while. She drank the borscht and let it warm her up from the inside. The dumplings were filled with something that might have been beef, but might have been a number of different things and she preferred not to think about it. Peppery and filling, and a little boozy, and she wanted to go back and get a hundred of them to take with her.

Inez was just outside the departure area for the taxis. Hers was in a couple of hours. Her bomb wounds were mostly under clothes, so no one paid her much mind. The terminal was in an area that used to be called Red Square. Some ancient buildings were there, with colorful, strange-shaped roofs, surrounded by other buildings that looked like solid blocks of concrete and just as plain.

She fought off the desire to get shitfaced. She was still on Earth, even if she wasn't right in the middle of Oslo. Better to wait until she was back on the rig. She wasn't even going to buy a bottle of vodka here, since she wasn't sure she could keep from drinking it all on the way. At least she had restocked her beer.

Lui had sent her a dozen messages since communications had been reestablished. It had made her promise that she wouldn't get into any trouble without it there to protect her. They were not lying when they said the automatons could get attached. She was glad to have someone to come home to, though. It said that her rig would be docked at the station above Moscow, ready to collect her.

She had yet to hear back from the Company, which seemed a bit odd. Maybe they were just trying to figure out the worst possible next job for her.

"These things give me willies," an older Russian man was saying, his accent on the thick side.

"Excuse me?" Inez said, picking up the bottle of water she had just paid extra for because they were on the taxi already.

"These taxis. They crawl up ropes that stretch for kilometers, but the ropes never break? No, of course the ropes break. But they don't ever tell you about that, do they?"

"They're monofilament nanotubes. They can't break."

"So they say, ya."

It was looking like this man was going to be her buddy on the taxi. He sat down next to her.

(Another sign that more people were trying to get to the planet than off of it was the lack of assigned seating.)

"No, I read an article about it before coming here. It's an infinitesimally small chance of happening, and if it did, you'd know about it because it would cause a ton of damage as it whipped back to Earth."

She actually had read an article on it as part of planning this whole... whatever the hell this had been.

The man held out his hand. "Piotr Minski."

"Trix Barbeau," she said, taking it. She had pulled that name completely out of thin air.

"Nyet, Inez."

Inez felt the bottom drop out of her stomach. "Excuse me?"

"Your friend Sara asked me to keep an eye on you. Discreetly."

"This is discreet?"

"I don't really do discreet."

She looked at the man closer now. He had a carefully ragged look, and not the haphazardly arranged look she had thought initially.

"I don't really do discreet, either."

"Yes, so I hear. Your friend was concerned after your robot told her what had happened. I have not been told, so anything secret should stay that way. I'm just here to make sure you get safely back to your ship."

She felt the gentle increase in gravity that meant they were ascending. She opened the water and took a sip.

"What is she doing?" Inez asked after a few minutes.

"Field analysis of a mining concern on Mercury."

Inez nodded and slowly blinked her eyes. "So, what is she really doing?"

Piotr tapped his finger on the side of his nose, then pointed at her smiling. "She said you were smart one." He never did tell her, though.

Inez sealed the medsuite and stripped. The scanners reached deep into her body and gave her a readout of the various injuries she had sustained. It also gave a cost per each one. She knew the bank chip had plenty on it, so she went for the deluxe package and a hair growth treatment for her far-too-exposed scalp. This was actually cheaper here than it would have been at a coiffurie.

She lay down on the treatment bed and the arms of the medsuite apparatus began knitting her back together. Her whole body was itching from the electrical fields, but she knew that moving her arms to scratch would have probably resulted in more injuries.

Work on her head took the longest. When the eardrum in her left ear was repaired, the suddenness of stereo sound almost made her cry. A day and a half without it and while she'd gotten by, everything had felt wrong.

There had been another concussion, as she'd expected. It was much smaller than the last two, but that was the final part of the treatment for her.

The whole thing took an hour and a half. She was tired of medsuites. And medbays. And med-chairs. She missed when just making sure she had the cannabid pain relievers was enough.

She got dressed, and could feel the fuzz already coming in on her head.

As she exited the medsuite, her earpiece chimed, and the rig said, "Mensaxe entrante." Short, to the point. Latinate words.

"Send the message through."

"Hey, Bee. I hope Piotr didn't talk your ear off the whole way up. He's a good guy, but once he gets started, oof. We can talk about everything that happened later. I know you want to, but don't come looking for me. Right now, there's too much going on.

"I found something a few years back. I can't tell you what it was, not right now, but it clarified a few things for me.

"I sent Lui a schematic for a decryption machine. It'll still take time to decrypt the data from that cube, but much less time than you would have taken on anything you currently have access to. I think it's important.

"Don't go doing anything stupid. I love you."

Inez felt like she'd been dropped into the middle of a long-running vid serial with no explanation of the plot. Not that she could just turn it off, of course.

Lui had parked the rig at a Company berth, using Inez's actual transponder signature. That made finding it pretty easy, all told. This was a larger berth than the one at Beehive, but most likely the one over Oslo would have been bigger still.

Given the L1 priority of delivering Bolivar, they were holding up letting her onto her Rig. An officious woman in a company-brown business suit and blue jay hair piled high on her head was standing behind a very neatly organized desk. She was in her late 30s, tall and very thin.

"You have a funny definition of keeping a low profile." She didn't show any sign of amusement.

"I was fine until the delivery was finalized," Inez countered. She had a growing pit in her stomach, suddenly. "It was the getting out that caused all the drama."

"We have heard from your package that he was very happy with your work. We are also pleased that we didn't have to get involved this time."

"Did you just know that or were you looking through my file?"

"Inez," the woman, Gael by the name plaque on her desk, continued, "you have a choice to make. You appear to be able to get in and out of dangerous situations. You completed an L1 delivery of contraband personnel and were not detained. We are impressed."

"You're praising me, but I feel like I'm about to get a beating. Why is that?"

"We occasionally have jobs that require a greater level of finesse and skill, and we need the right people to handle them." Gael was looking at multiple pads at the same time, each with a different readout that Inez couldn't decipher. "Cargoists like you are rare, and if the incident at the waystation hadn't brought you to our attention, we likely never would have known."

"Am I having a different conversation than you are?"

"We will call on you when one of these jobs comes up. For now, you have earned a little time away. Find somewhere to go and put your feet up."

"I'm not going to have any right of refusal on these jobs, am I?"

"Of course not."

Inez sighed. Time to get going, then.

Lui greeted Inez as she entered the rig. The mechanotron looked no worse for wear, which is not something Inez could say about herself at this point.

"Bud, can you take us away from here? I don't care where, right now."

A short clip of a girl saying "You got it!" popped up in front of her. She chuckled and batted it closed. She headed to her bunk, managed to get her boots off and let the jumpsuit fall around her feet.

She collapsed into the bed and was soon deep in a dreamless sleep. Lui trundled in, turned off the light and pulled the blanket up over Inez's shoulders before slipping back into box form next to the bed.

Acknowledgements

Once again, to try and pass off this book as only being my creation start to finish is a disservice to myself and to the many people who helped me along the way.

First, to my betas Maria, Patrick, Caroline, and (always) Mary Ellen, thanks for catching all of the little things I would have missed.

My editor was again Kat Howard, who is fantastic and always knows exactly the right changes to make Inez's story stronger.

This has been a strange time, stuck at home so much that even an introvert needed human contact. Thanks to the Speculative Writers Discord and the Writers Block Discord servers for the support and the cheering up.

As ever, thanks to you, dear reader, for making this all worthwhile. Look for more fun with Inez in the coming months!

JS (Jeff) Carter Gilson
August 2020
http://www.jscartergilson.com/

Translation

The computer is still on the fritz, so here's some more translations for you.

Page 1:
"E i ai sau valaauga ulufale." Samoan. "You have an incoming call."
"Sie haben einen eingehenden Anruf." German. "You have an incoming call."

Page 12:
"Yebo, nduna." Zulu. "Yes, sir."

Page 90:
"Prešli smo marsovski obod. Upočasni na petindvajsetsto kilometrov na sekundo." Slovenian. "We crossed the Martian perimeter. It slows down to twenty-five kilometers per second."

Page 100
"Aš nežinau, apie ką jūs kalbate." Lithuanian. "I don't know what you're talking about."

Page 104
" បាទ ប្រកា ន ក្រុម។" Khmer. "Yes, Captain."

Page 127
"Mensaxe entrante." Galician. "Incoming message."

https://www.jscartergilson.com/

www.ingramcontent.com/pod-product-compliance
Lightning Source LLC
Chambersburg PA
CBHW022033170626
46808CB00003B/1175